THE MASQUE OF THE RED DEATH

BearManor Media
P.O. Box 1129
Duncan, OK 73534-1129

Phone: 580-252-3547
Fax: 814-690-1559

www.bearmanormedia.com

The Masque of the Red Death by Elsie Lee
First published as a Lancer Book -1964
The Masque of the Red Death produced by
American International Pictures, 1964
Roger Corman Interview ©2013 Lawrence French
Photographs - Lawrence French & Philip J. Riley

Edited and book design by Philip J. Riley ©2013

The Nightmares Series is being published to preserve original movie tie-in novels that were printed in the 1950s and 1960s on the old style pulp paper. We hope these reprints will allow them to last into the new century.

THE MASQUE
OF THE RED DEATH

By
ELSIE LEE

From the screenplay by Charles Beaumont & R. Wright Campbell

Philip J. Riley's

NIGHTMARE SERIES

BearManor Media

6418-P-2

Deliverance . . . or Doom?

"The day of deliverance is at hand." That was the prophecy of the mysterious man cloaked in red. But the villagers had little time for rejoicing. For a few scant hours later, the people were dying of that grimmest of all plagues—the Red Death!

And within the castle that ruled this desolated land, even eerier events were happening . . . as the purity of the lovely Francesca battled the evil of Price Prospero . . . and unearthly forces gathered for a mad, grim masquerade!

Roger Corman directs Jane Asher and Vincent Price.

ROGER CORMAN

interviewed on

THE MASQUE OF THE RED DEATH

By Lawrence French

LAWRENCE FRENCH: You had mentioned before that the reason you finally made *The Masque of the Red Death* was because you had used up all the other suitable Poe stories. Yet, there were certainly several good Poe stories you could have utilized, such as Ligeia and The Gold-Bug, weren't there?

ROGER CORMAN: Yes, there was other Poe material, but what it amounted to was out of the remaining Poe stories, the best one was The Masque of the Red Death. I always felt it was one of Poe's finest stories. But because Ingmar Bergman's *The Seventh Seal* had come out a few years earlier and had some elements that were similar to *The Masque of the Red Death*, I would always choose something else. I thought people would say I was taking from Bergman—even though I was working from a 19th century source. So each time we did another Poe film that choice would come up. Finally, I felt that of the remaining Poe stories, I really liked *The Masque of the Red Death* the best. So whether or not there were some similarities to *The Seventh Seal*, I simply decided to make *The Masque of the Red Death*. I kept moving The Masque of the Red Death back, because of the similarities, but it was really an artificial reason in my mind. Poe obviously wrote *The Masque of the Red Death* in the 19th century, and Bergman wrote *The Seventh Seal* in the 20th, so Poe could hardly be accused of taking from Bergman. So finally, I just went ahead and decided to make it.

LAWRENCE FRENCH: Of course, when *The Masque of the Red Death* came out, your predictions came true. Some critics accused you of plagiarizing Bergman!

ROGER CORMAN: As a matter of fact, I was trying to work in the opposite direction. I was trying to stay away. However, you're led to certain solutions to problems that are the best solutions. You say, all right, this is the best way to do the scene. I have no reason to do it badly, just so it's different from something that has been done before.

LAWRENCE FRENCH: It's also been suggested that Luis Buñuel has influenced you, especially because his films had so many dream sequences. However, in Buñuel's *Belle de Jour* (made in 1966) there is a sequence where Catherine Deneuve is asleep in a coffin and suddenly wakes up. I thought it was very similar to the scene in *The Masque of the Red Death*, where Jane Asher finds Vincent Price asleep in a coffin and he suddenly opens his eyes. So maybe you had an influence on Buñuel!

ROGER CORMAN: I doubt if Buñuel stole from me. And I don't think I ever stole from Buñuel, because I hadn't seen that many of his films when I was making the Poe pictures, although I did see *Belle de Jour.*

LAWRENCE FRENCH: It's not that you stole from Bergman or Bunuel, but that they may have influenced you, just as Jean Renoir and Alfred Hitchcock influenced Francois Truffaut. In fact,Ingmar Bergman commented about the influence on his work in 1960, saying: "Either you are original or you are not. I would say that the fact that we (filmmakers) influence each other—we give to and we borrow from and we experience from all art disciplines, both vertically and horizontally—that goes without saying. But this thing about offering something entirely new at all costs, that is plain silly."

ROGER CORMAN: Yes, exactly, and I think there is a common filmic language, so the images are in all of us. There is also a certain solution to situations. You may want to portray something in a scene, and often there is a very clear way in which to do it best. This is too elementary an analogy, but if you ask two people how much three plus three is, and they both answer six, neither one is stealing from the other; but that is the answer to the question.

LAWRENCE FRENCH: Did you meet Ingmar Bergman when you picked up *Cries and Whispers* for distribution by New World Pictures in 1971?

ROGER CORMAN: Yes, I did meet Bergman, and he was rather formal, but a very intelligent and quite an intense man. He was a little bit quiet, but that's probably because English is not his first language. If we had been speaking in Swedish, maybe he would not have been quite as quiet. I told him the first film of his I had ever seen was *The Seventh Seal* and that I admired it greatly. I think it is a wonderful picture. We mostly talked in general though, and I liked him very much.

LAWRENCE FRENCH: Did you ever attempt to distribute any of Luis Buñuel's films through New World?

Roger Corman discusses the script with Hazel Court & Jane Asher.

ROGER CORMAN: Yes, as a matter of fact, we almost handled the distribution of Buñuel's last picture, *That Obscure Object of Desire* (1977), but at the last minute they went with another company. I actually saw more of Buñuel's films after I had stopped directing, and started New World. Of the Buñuel films that I have seen, they have all been very good and I think he is a really brilliant director, but at the time I was directing, my favorite director was, and still may be, Sergei Eisenstein (the Russian director of *Potemkin* and *Ivan the Terrible*). I also like the work of Hitchcock, of John Ford, of Howard Hawks, of Akira Kurosawa and of Ingmar Bergman. I especially like the work of Bergman very much.

LAWRENCE FRENCH: Since you've said you like the work of Luis Buñuel, I want to get your opinion on this statement he made:
    "The cinema seems to have been invented to express the life of the subconscious. A film is like an involuntary imitation of a dream."

ROGER CORMAN: I agree totally with that. I think film is probably the best medium we have to show the images of the unconscious mind. We dream in images and watching a movie is really an experience very closely related to the workings of the unconscious mind. Now in the Poe films I was dealing with the unconscious much more overtly than in other types of pictures, but I still think the feeling is there in all of my films.

LAWRENCE FRENCH: What are some of the horror films you've remembered or have admired?

ROGER CORMAN: I liked many of the German silent films, like *The Cabinet of Dr. Caligari* and *Nosferatu*. I also liked Werner Herzog's remake of *Nosferatu*. I liked James Whale's original *Frankenstein* and the horror films Val Lewton made in the forties at RKO. I also thought Wes Craven's *The Nightmare on Elm Street* was outstanding. The idea that creatures from one's own dreams could kill you is a truly classical concept.

LAWRENCE FRENCH: Why did you go to England to make *The Masque of the Red Death*? Since it was all shot in the studio, couldn't you have made it just as easily in Hollywood?

ROGER CORMAN: That was simply a matter of economics. AIP had a co-production deal with Anglo-Amalgamated in England, so Jim and Sam suggested we go to England to make *The Masque of the Red Death*. All the Poe films had done extremely well in England and there was also a subsidy from the British government called the Eady plan. That was before any other country had a subsidy. I think there was a tax on theater admissions and that money was reserved for pictures that were made in England. We were quite happy to go over, because it meant we would be able to increase our budget for *The Masque of the Red Death* which was going to require more time and money than we had spent on any of the earlier Poe pictures. The budget is determined so much by your schedule and for *The Masque of the Red Death* we had five weeks. In Hollywood, from the beginning to the end of the cycle, all of the Poe pictures were done in three weeks. With 25 days I got a bigger look, but I'd say that five weeks in England was the equivalent to four weeks in the United States, simply because the English crews worked slower. They did very good work, but were very slow in comparison to American crews. We broke at eleven in the morning and also at mid-afternoon for tea, so while it was very civilized, we didn't get quite as much work done.

LAWRENCE FRENCH: Of course, having a whole new crew to become familiar with probably meant you'd be working slower as well, since in America you had used the same crew on most of the Poe films, which no doubt helped to speed things up. Vincent Price said it was like having a little stock company.

ROGER CORMAN: Yes, the fact that I retained most of the crew from picture to picture did help. It helped not only on the Poe films, but on other films they made with me, as well. What happened was on my first film as a director I hired a group of people, and on my second film I hired the best people back. Then, on my third picture, I hired the best from that group, so after a very short number of films, I really had the best people I could find in each position. That gave me two benefits: First, I had the best people in each position, and second, they knew each other and began to work together as a team, like basketball players. First you get a group of all-stars, and when they practice together, they get that much better. In fact, they became known as the "Corman crew," and when they weren't working with me, AIP would sometimes hire them out as a unit, as they did when I turned down *The Comedy of Terrors*. I look back at that whole period as a very good working time. We were all friends, everybody liked each other, and there was a great spirit of camaraderie. They were all very good technicians and they rose above the level of technique, to help with the artistic endeavor as a whole. Now, in England, I didn't have that same kind of camaraderie with the crew, possibly because I was an American and seen as something of an outsider.

LAWRENCE FRENCH: I read a report in *Sight and Sound* that you became upset at your English crew during the shooting of *The Masque of the Red Death* when the lights went out during a shot.

ROGER CORMAN: I don't think the lights ever went out on a shot, but you do have to finish at specific times. The English crews are bound very rigidly by union rules. It's a major problem to get overtime. You have to announce to them before two in the afternoon if you want overtime, and then they call a

Vincent Price and Patrick Magee
Skip Martin as Hop-Toad

union meeting to decide whether or not you're going to get it. I got it every time I asked for it, but they had to call a meeting anyway. I've heard of directors who asked for overtime, and the crew would say "no." I got along pretty well with the crew, although they knew I was somewhat critical of the slow pace. It became a slight, running sore joke.

LAWRENCE FRENCH: One advantage of being in England was the quality of supporting actors you could cast. Did you decide on Patrick Magee after using him in *Dementia 13*, the Francis Ford Coppola picture you produced?

ROGER CORMAN: No, I had first used Patrick Magee in *The Young Racers*, a film I made in Europe. After we had finished shooting on *The Young Racers*, I backed Francis Coppola in making *Dementia 13* in Ireland, utilizing several of the same cast and crew whom I had used on *The Young Racers*. But I had seen some of Patrick Magee's English pictures, and I thought he was a very good character actor. He could find these strange little quirks to his character, which he would bring out during his performance, making it a richer and more fully rounded characterization. I also thought he brought a real sense of menace and the macabre to his role as Alfredo.

LAWRENCE FRENCH: Did Charles Beaumont and R. Wright Campbell actually collaborate on the script for *The Masque of the Red Death*?

ROGER CORMAN: No, they did not. Chuck Beaumont had written the first draft of Masque, but I was not totally satisfied with it. I had just come off a picture, *The Secret Invasion* that I had made in Yugoslavia, which Bob Campbell had written, so Bob came to London with me where we worked on the re-write of *The Masque of the Red Death*. I always thought Bob did an excellent job on the re-write. At the time Chuck was in the United States and was very ill, so he was not able to come to England or do a re-write.

LAWRENCE FRENCH: From Charles Beaumont's previous work, I imagine he came up with the idea of making Prince Prospero a Satanist.

ROGER CORMAN: Yes, that was in Chuck's first draft, and then Bob Campbell introduced the sub-plot of the dwarf, from another Poe story, Hop-Frog. That was Bob's idea, which was not in Chuck's original script.

LAWRENCE FRENCH: Skip Martin, the actor who played Hop-Toad, was marvelous, but the child actress who played the tiny dancer was quite obviously dubbed.

ROGER CORMAN: That was a casting problem I found that we just couldn't solve. We needed a female dwarf who would look beautiful and who

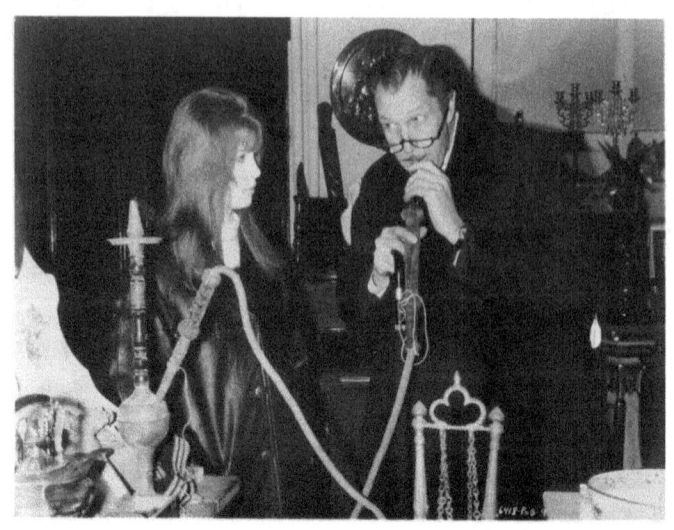

Vincent Price and Jane Asher spent a day off from shooting The Masque of Red Death to tour London's famed Petticoat Lane. Here in an antique shop, Price instructs Ms. Asher on how to smoke a hooka pipe

Jane Asher clowns with Nigel Green - (Note sword in Green)

could also dance, and we simply couldn't find one in London. Finally, the only solution that presented itself was to use an attractive little girl who could dance and would also be the right height. Then with make-up, we tried to make her look as old as possible.

LAWRENCE FRENCH: Did you ask a writer named John Carter—who you apparently met in Arkansas while making *The Intruder*—to write a script for *The Masque of the Red Death*?

ROGER CORMAN: Yes, I did. I don't remember that situation exactly, but I think the script he wrote simply did not work out the way I wanted, so I put it away. I cannot tell you anything else about it, except that I didn't use it.

LAWRENCE FRENCH: Did you also ask Robert Towne to write a draft of *The Masque of the Red Death*?

ROGER CORMAN: I don't recall that, but it might have happened, because Bob Towne wrote the second Poe film I did in England, *Tomb of Ligeia*.

LAWRENCE FRENCH: I presume you didn't ask Alex Gordon to write a script for *The Masque of the Red Death*, because after the movie came out, Alex Gordon sued AIP, claiming the film was based on a screenplay he had written previously, although he lost his case in court.

ROGER CORMAN: That's right, but that was really something between AIP and Alex, because Alex is a friend of mine and a really nice guy. But I never saw the script Alex had written, so it had no influence on me whatsoever.

15

LAWRENCE FRENCH: The dialogue at the masque between Prospero and Death was really quite effective, because it could have easily become rather absurd.

ROGER CORMAN: Yes, you're riding a very fine line there. I think working with Bob Campbell helped, because he had a very good ear for dialogue. I think of the writers I worked with on the Poe films, Dick Matheson was very good, as was Bob Campbell, and of course, Robert Towne, who did *The Tomb Of Ligeia*. I was most pleased with their work.

LAWRENCE FRENCH: You mentioned that you felt the Poe films were becoming too similar to one another, yet when you went to England to make *The Masque of the Red Death* and *Tomb of Ligeia* I found they were both quite unique. They have much better acting, as well as very literate scripts, which seem to capture more of the flavor of Poe—perhaps because they're a culmination of your ideas. In retrospect, I think they are your two best Poe films.

ROGER CORMAN: As a matter of fact, so do I. I think just being in England and working with a different crew, stimulated me to function differently. I was also making a conscious effort to make the films differently. I was specifically trying to grow and to change. So on *Masque* I had a slightly different lighting style, and then when I went back to England to shoot *Tomb of Ligeia* I finally made the decision to break out of the studio walls and photograph the real world.

LAWRENCE FRENCH: Vincent Price said that since you weren't allowed to bring any of your American crew over to work on *The Masque of the Red Death*, you had to give an English art director credit, but you actually used Daniel Haller.

ROGER CORMAN: That's right. I had Dan come over and Dan's wife Kinta had rented a really nice house in Knightsbridge and I lived with them while we were shooting *Masque of the Red Death*. We had some really great times there. We'd have dinners and people would come floating in from the set, Vincent and all of the actors. Bob Campbell who had worked on the script was also there, so it was a sort of general meeting place, like the Hemingway thing, a movable feast, except it was just moving from day to day but always staying in the same house. But when Dan and I first went to the studio, we went through it and found we could adapt some of the sets left over from major English historical pictures. Dan was able to adapt and build our sets around existing flats that really gave us the best look we ever had, because we had sets from multi-million dollar pictures. I think they were from *Becket* and *A Man for All Seasons?*

LAWRENCE FRENCH: It couldn't have been *A Man for All Seasons,* because that was made in 1966 after you shot *Masque of the Red Death*. But in England you were not credited as producer of *The Masque of the Red Death*. George Willoughby was listed as the producer.

ROGER CORMAN: That was simply because we needed to credit a British producer, due to the subsidy we got from the Eady plan.

LAWRENCE FRENCH: The set design for *The Masque of the Red Death* follows the description in Poe's story quite closely for the multicolored suite of seven rooms, although you reduced them to only four in the movie.

ROGER CORMAN: Yes, since we had to vary the stories to a great extent, whenever we could we tried to keep the set design as faithful to Poe's original story as was possible. But in adapting *The Masque of the Red Death* we had a story that was only five pages long, therefore the concept of the multicolored chambers was a conscious decision I made to remain as close to the description in Poe's story as we could get. Danny Haller designed those rooms as a series of U-sets that were all built next to each other with a door between them so I could dolly from one room to another. So I started in the first room and then just went down the line, following Vincent as Prince Prospero and Jane Asher and I would stop in each room and have a close-up as they were talking to each other before I'd continue onto the next room. I always liked that sequence, as I felt it was one of the best scenes in the film, although the biggest scene was the dance of death at the end of the picture.

LAWRENCE FRENCH: *House of Usher* begins with Philip arriving through a forest that has been blackened by a plague, and ends with a blaze that destroys the house. Conversely, *The Masque of the Red Death* begins with the village being burned to the ground, and ends with Prince Prospero's castle being overcome by the red death. Was that a conscious decision to reverse the order of the catastrophes, or was it just a way of getting *The Masque of the Red Death* off to a dramatic start?

ROGER CORMAN: To a certain extent that was conscious. Fire figures very heavily in Poe's work, and I think fire, and the ocean, as well as a number of other things, are very important to people unconsciously. Fire is a symbol of destruction as well as purification. I used fire consciously in a number of the Poe films, as a primary elemental force. Fire, water and even the plague are all perfectly natural phenomenon that can symbolize the powers of nature. So when I was preparing the Poe films, I went very deeply into Freudian theory.

LAWRENCE FRENCH: In the pressbook for *The Masque of the Red Death,* you are quoted as saying, "the most chilling moment of any horror film will usually occur in a long corridor, where some character is either running away from, or approaching some unspecified object of unparalleled terror." Could you explain your reasoning behind that?

ROGER CORMAN: There you have symbolism, which is very sexual. My theory was that the corridor represented the vagina. It's a moment of both anticipation and horror, where you have a kind of fear—attraction combination. You don't know what's at the end of the corridor, it might be frightening, but at the same time you're irresistibly drawn towards it. In general, I thought of the house as a woman's body. So often in Poe and in other horror films, everything takes place in a house or a castle. And I thought of the doorways, the passages and the windows, as being symbolic of the vagina.

LAWRENCE FRENCH: So what was the Freudian significance of the corridor in terms of the psychological theories that you were working with?

ROGER CORMAN: I felt that horror was, to a certain extent, a re-creation of childhood fears: early fears of the dark and early concepts of sexuality. For instance, a small child might be in the house late at night. Maybe he's just come out of a nightmare and he wakes up alone and afraid. His parents are down the hall and its dark and stormy outside. He starts wandering through the dark hallways, looking for his parents, so the corridor has many meanings, which will apply to that. Then as the child goes down the hall towards his parent's bedroom he hears noises; the bed is shaking and there might be cries of passion, so it will also apply to an early thought of sex, in which the corridor represents the vagina. And if it's thundering and lightning outside, that adds to the child's fear, because those are things he doesn't quite understand. To a large degree, the world outside is greater than the child—things out there are beyond his control and they frighten him. Later, his parents may try to explain these things to him as perfectly natural phenomena, but the explanation is usually only partially successful, because the fear the child has experienced has already made a deep and lasting impression on his subconscious mind. Then, as the child grows up, most of these childhood fears are sublimated, but some of them remain—only now they are buried deep within his unconscious mind. So what I was trying to do in these pictures was to take the mind back to those early childhood fears—to the very young child.

LAWRENCE FRENCH: Did you have any kind of similar experience, which frightened you as a child?

ROGER CORMAN: No, not to my recollection. I think one of the essentials of the theory is that you bury these frightening events from your childhood into your unconscious mind. So you don't remember them consciously. And in trying to go back to that early stage and recreate these childhood fears, I felt the best way to accomplish it was by a slow build-up of suspense, followed by a sudden shock effect. The surprise of the shock effect helps to momentarily break through and reach the unconscious mind. But in order to work correctly, it has to happen very quickly; otherwise the conscious mind will recognize what is happening and make a correction.

LAWRENCE FRENCH: That actually relates to Carl Jung's work, since you are dealing with the collective unconscious of the audience.

ROGER CORMAN: Yes, the unconscious minds of most people raised in Western civilization have many similarities. We've all been raised in basically the same way, so it was an attempt to reach the universal ground that exists in every-one's unconscious—which is a very difficult thing to do. It's an attempt to create in your conscious mind, what only exists in your unconscious. So I was using a little bit of Jung, particularly the archetype, but dealing primarily with Freud.

LAWRENCE FRENCH: How carefully would you want the scriptwriter to detail some of your Freudian ideas, for instance, in the corridor sequence in *Masque of the Red Death* where Jane Asher is wandering around the castle late at night and discovers Vincent Price asleep in a coffin. There's absolutely no dialogue in the scene, it's just the camera, music and sound effects.

ROGER CORMAN: It would say this in the script: "Francesca wanders through the castle corridors," with a brief description of the action in the scene.

19

Since I'd already worked with the writer on the script, we'd put just that in and I'd work with that. There was no justification for putting more than that in the

After cinematographer Nicholas Roeg worked on Masque of the Red Death, he photographed several period films, including Far From the Madding Crowd. Here Roeg is seen in costume as an extra on that film, in a hat quite similar to the one Vincent Price would wear in Corman's final Poe movie, The Tomb of Ligeia.

script, because I knew what I was going to do. I think it's a total waste of time to put long descriptions of shots in the script. There may be certain things I want to include in the script, to remind me of effects I'd like to achieve in a sequence like that, but we don't need to go beyond that. I would generally work very closely with the writer and if he tried to write out in great detail a sequence like that, I'd say, "it's all right to put in certain concepts we want in this sequence, but there's no need to put in any more than that." I prefer that from the screenwriter, because it is generally not the screenwriter's job to pick the shots. That's really the director's job. Writers who put in a lot of shots and things like that are really kidding themselves, because they generally don't have the experience to do it, or they haven't seen the set. There is no way to specify shots with any degree of accuracy until you've seen the sets or the location. Usually, it wasn't until after the script was written that I could work with the art director on the layout of the sets, and the layout of the sets would determine the shot plan. So the whole shot plan for all of those kinds of sequences would only be determined after the script was written.

LAWRENCE FRENCH: What about suggestions from the cameraman. Did Nicolas Roeg give you any suggestions for camera angles?

ROGER CORMAN: No, I generally set my own shots. I think of the

20

cameraman the way the English do. They call him a lighting cameraman. His primary job is the lights. I'd say that 95% of the shots in my films come from me. The other 5% will be an idea or modification from the cameraman. To me the director's job is to set the shots, the cameraman's job is to light the scene. What I will do is have a meeting with the cameraman, during which I will talk about the mood and the style I want to shoot in and the effect I'm trying to find. Then it's the cameraman's job to get that mood and get that lighting. Working with Floyd Crosby and Nic Roeg, that was essentially their job. I considered them both to be extremely good cameramen. They were able to get on low budgets and fast schedules, very intricate lighting. It was very sophisticated lighting for that type of film.

LAWRENCE FRENCH: Frankly, I think the camerawork in Masque of the Red Death not only stands up against the bigger budgeted films released in 1964, like *My Fair Lady*, *Mary Poppins* and *Becket* (which all were nominated for best cinematography Oscars), but is actually better than many of them!

ROGER CORMAN: Yes, I think Nicolas Roeg did a truly brilliant job on *The Masque of the Red Death*. He even won an award for the picture at some European film festival. The reason I hired Nic, was due to the English labor laws, which wouldn't allow me to use Floyd Crosby. At the time, Nic was a young English cameraman, who had been a 2nd unit cameraman on *Lawrence of Arabia*, but he had really only done a couple of pictures. After I'd seen some of his work and talked with him, I felt he would be able to bring the kind of interesting chiaroscuro quality that I was looking for in the lighting and the sets.

LAWRENCE FRENCH: Despite the gorgeous color cinematography, I felt that the masque itself was not a complete success.

ROGER CORMAN: You're right when you say the masque was not a complete success, because I felt that myself. What it amounted to was there was not enough time. We were shooting just before Christmas, with some sort of stop date. We had a 25-day schedule and it could not be 26. The dancing troupe was committed to do some Christmas pantomime, so there was no way to go an extra day. I really needed more time for the masque sequence. I shot the whole masque sequence in one day, which would have been ample time in the U.S. I was able to shoot the whole pit and the pendulum sequence in less than a day in the United States. But the English crews simply could not get it. I knew that the English crews were slower, but I still felt I could get the masque sequence in one day. When we got to it, there was no way to get the whole sequence in one day. I've always felt that no film is perfect, there are a number of flaws in any film, particularly in my films, but the greatest flaw in *The Masque of the Red Death* is that the masque itself was not completely realized. If I had gotten that extra day, I think I could have done more with it.

21

LAWRENCE FRENCH: Actually, it would seem like an incredibly complicated sequence to shoot in a single day. You also had to work with a choreographer, so it's unfortunate you couldn't have had that extra day.

ROGER CORMAN: Yes, I regretted that as well. Now I said the masque itself took one whole day, but there were other scenes leading up to the masque and around it that were shot before that day. I can't remember the whole sequence of shots, but I do remember that the actual dancing sections where shot in one day. However, there were scenes where people would come out of the masque and then come back in, that were not shot on that day.

LAWRENCE FRENCH: One of those scenes was when Vincent Price throws jewels down to the masked revelers. He said he started down the stairs and tripped over his long robe and knocked himself out!

ROGER CORMAN: I don't remember that. It might have happened, but it was a long time ago, so I don't remember exactly. One thing I do remember is the assassination of President Kennedy. That happened just a few days after we started shooting (on November 22, 1963). It was a great shock to both Vincent and myself because we were both strong supporters of President Kennedy and we were far from home. I remember on the day of the President's funeral, we stopped shooting briefly and we had a moment of silence to honor the President.

LAWRENCE FRENCH: I think one of the key themes of the Poe films is summed up by Prospero's line, "How easily a man's mind can be controlled and twisted." In most of the Poe films one character's mind succumbs to someone who has a stronger will. It's certainly at the center of *Ligeia*.

ROGER CORMAN: There again, it's connected to a large extent to my interpretation of horror, to the workings of the unconscious mind and to Poe himself. I think that one of the most horrifying things is the concept of loss of control. The fact that we cannot control our own destinies—whether it's a spirit, or a ghost or some other force that takes control of our minds and bodies. I think that's a very horrifying concept, and as a result it flows through all of the Poe films.

LAWRENCE FRENCH: Prospero goes on to tell Jane Asher, "That somewhere in the human mind is the key to our existence. My ancestors tried to open the door that separates us from our creator."

ROGER CORMAN: That's part of the basic question Prospero is seeking an answer to. It's a common human desire to discover what is out there in the world around us. It's really a desire to know the unknown.

LAWRENCE FRENCH: In *Masque of the Red Death* you seemed to be exploring the whole concept of death and allowed a more artistic side to dominate, as opposed to the kinds of thrills AIP wanted for their core horror audience. As a result, Sam Arkoff complained about your "arty-farty approach" and he felt the movie wasn't scary enough.

ROGER CORMAN: Yes, it was really not what AIP wanted, so when Sam said *Masque of the Red Death* wasn't as scary as the previous pictures, I think that is a legitimate statement. The fault may have been mine. I was becoming more interested in the Poe films as expressions of the unconscious mind, rather than as pure horror films. Actually, they were never pure horror films, they were a certain type of film that had horror in them. So *Masque of the Red Death* was a little more philosophical and there was very little violence, per se. We were dealing with the plague, so it was a fear of death itself—not of any physical violence or torture. As a result, the horror content in the picture did diminish.

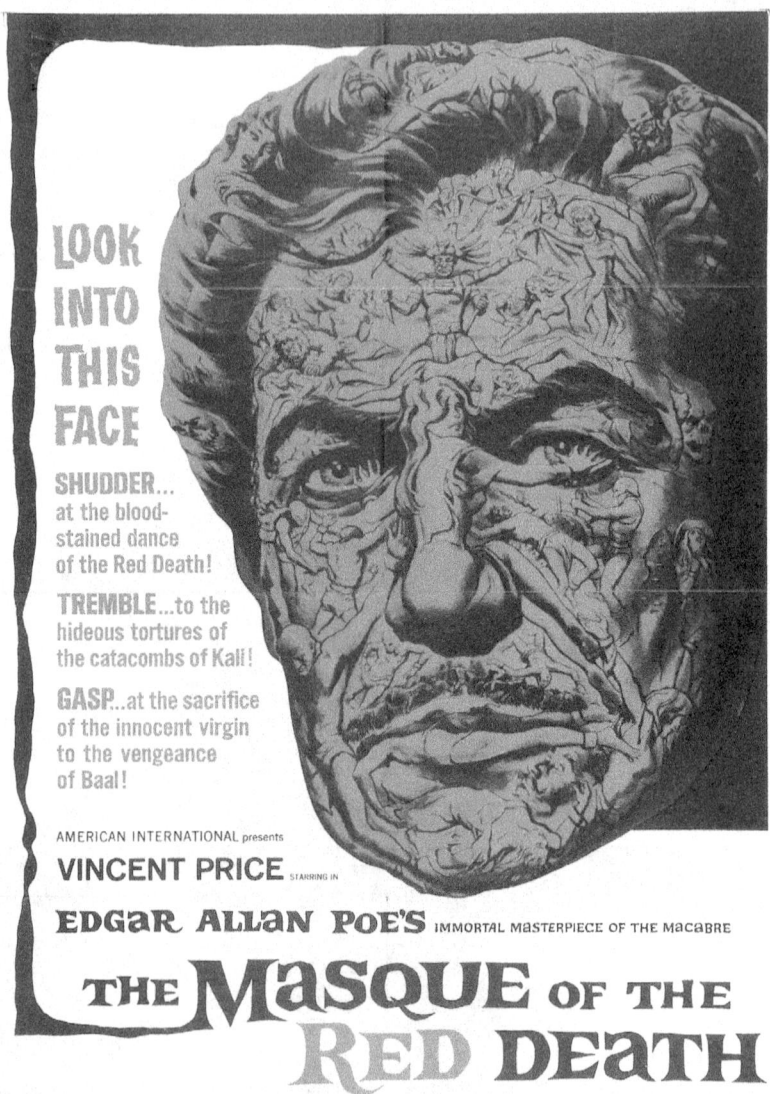

Chapter I

ON the eve of All Saint's Day, in the year of Our Lord 1548, the village crone of Estaban went out to search for firewood. Her name was Concetta, and neither she nor anyone else in Estaban knew how old she was. Sometimes she thought she had once been married, and occasionally she had a dim memory of children, but if it were true and not merely a dream, they were all gone now. Concetta had been living alone for so many years she no longer bothered to count the days.

In their way and as they could spare time from the difficulties of their own lives, the people of Estaban were kind to old Concetta. Whenever her rickety thatched cottage threatened to collapse entirely, some of the men would prop it up again; a few of the younger women spared an hour or so to help with her share of the community tillage. Quite often the village youngsters brought her a few bits of firewood, but now that winter was approaching, the children were filling their family woodboxes first. Concertta quite understood. She had been going out every day, gathering whatever she could find.

I would not be enough to last through the winter, of course, because she moved so very slowly and could carry only a small armload. She'd gleaned the last bit of bark or tiny twig from the places nearest her cottage, going farther afield each day—and it was still not going to be enough.

So today she would have to try the hill. It would be very tiring, and chilly as well, because the hill was steep and stark, with no shelter from the strong wind that swept across its summit. Concetta wrapped the worn shawl about her as tightly as possible, and made her way laboriously to the outskirts of the village. Perhaps, after all, she might find enough brush and twigs without having to go quite to the top, and with this faint hope in her heart, Concetta kept her faded old eyes fixed to the ground.

With infinite patience, she crept forward, bending painfully to collect a piece of tree bark her, a fallen branch there, but it was a pitiful armload. The children had been before her, of course, and had taken the best. On she went, stopping once in a while to rest and scan the ground about her; *nothing* must be overlooked . . .

In her preoccupation, she had almost reached the top of the hill and the cold wind was piercing through her wretched thin shawl. Concetta shivered uncontrollably and very nearly turned back—but just *there,* to the side of the great gnarled tree that crowned the hill, thrusting its naked limbs to the lowering sky, she spied a really worthwhile piece of firewood. I was a full limb of the tree, blown off in the wild gales of the past few days since the children had finished gathering, or they would have had it.

Eagerly, Concetta hobbled toward it. If only it were not too heavy for her to drag down the hill, what a fire it would make! Dimly, she thought she would save it for Christmas. How better to celebrate Our Saviour's birth! She was past the big tree, ignoring the deep shadows it cast, when a voice said, "Grandmother!"

Concetta gasped involuntarily, clutching the armload of twigs to her pounding heart. Slowly, she turned and peered about, until the voice said again, "Grandmother!"

It came from the obscurity beyond the great tree, and Concetta's fright ebbed away, for this was a voice of great weariness that she had a sudden flash of childhood memory: once she had had a father whose voice had been tender, gentle, loving. Concetta was conscious of warmth within her, even as the cruel gusts penetrated her shawl. She took a few tentative steps forward, and gradually her eyes discerned a hooded figure, seated in the shadow of the tree.

Tremulously, she put a hand to her mouth to still the quivering of her lips; there was no doubt that this was a very holy man. His monk's habit was of a rich deep red that made a spot of intense color against the grayness of the landscape. Concetta could not see his face beneath the hood; it was only her eagerness for the fine tree limb that had caused her to pass him, unnoticing.

Now, as she shuffled forward another few steps, she saw that he leaned against the tree trunk and was playing cards. Over his shoulder, Concetta observed the fine thin-boned hands manipulating the cards with grace and delicacy, gathering them together and mixing with incredible speed . . . only to lay them forth upon the ground before him, pondering over each separate card with solemn concentration.

Concetta had heard of playing cards. They were used by lords and ladies, kings and princes, to while away time in the palaces. Of course, she had never actually seen such cards. An old peasant woman had few enough hours to accomplish her work, let alone any time to waste. Breathless and awed, she peered at the cards with their strange symbols and painted faces. What a tale to be told in the village! There was even one face that might have been a portrait of Prince Prospero, to whom the village owed allegiance. Concetta's lips firmed into a taut line of hatred, while the hooded figure set that card in the center and pored over it for a long moment, before slowing continuing his game.

"Come closer, grandmother," the deep voice commanded, tenderly.

Insensibly, Concetta dropped her firewood and hobbled forward, hypnotized by that strange sense of warmth. She paused, respectfully, just behind his shoulder, while one hand reached within the folds of the red robe and drew forth a fresh rose. It was pure white, perfectly shaped, nodding gracefully on its green stem, and as his hand held it before him momentarily, a wave of its delicious fragrance came to the old woman.

Concetta closed her eyes and breathed deeply. "It is a gift for you, grandmother," the voice told her gently. Concetta opened her eyes and stared, half-frightened once more. A fine fresh rose at this time of year? And for her? What manner of being would give a rose to an old peasant woman: an angel—or, perhaps, a devil?

As she gazed confusedly at the rose, his other hand stretched out to hover over the flower, the fingers seem to sprinkle, to beckon—and before her eyes, red drops bedewed the white petals until the rose was as richly crimson as the monk's robe. Now the hand extended it to her, and while she hesitated, the voice spoke again.

"Take this to your village, and tell the people the day of their deliverance is at hand."

In response to the loving tones of that most beautiful voice, Concetta's hand went forward to accept the glowing flower. Wonderingly, she looked at it—bent her head to breathe deep of the perfume—and a tremulous smile touched her withered lips. Reverently she pressed it to her breast, and sought for words.

"I thank your Eminence," she faltered in her reedy old voice, but the figure merely gestured gently toward the path back to the village and returned to laying out the cards, one by one, most deliberately and carefully, in a sort of circle about that central card which resembled Prince Prospero—but every now and then placing a single card to one side.

Old Concetta wavered briefly, but she could remember nothing more of courtesy to say, so she turned and hobbled away as quickly as her rheumatic legs would carry her, forgetting the fine tree limb that would have celebrated the Christ Child's birthday. At the edge of the summit plateau, she recalled her manners and turned, unsteadily essaying a curtsey and crossing herself reverently, but the figure neither looked nor made any sign of recognition, and Concetta turned back to the downward path.

Picking her way over the stones and ruts, the occasional exposed gnarled roots, Concetta stumbled along in the gathering darkness. Still she felt within her that strange and wonderful warmth; still she held the beautiful fresh rose and inhaled its sweetness.

It was only as she made what speed her old legs could manage along the single street of Estaban, and called out in her cracked voice to summon the inhabitant, that she dimly recalled *why* she had been on the hill in the first place, or thought of the lost firewood.

"Look!" she said. "See!" Proudly she held the rose high over her head. "A holy man gave it to me—on the hill—with a message for all of you." For a moment, she faltered again. What was it the monk had said? She *must* remember his words, she must . . . Concetta closed her eyes in agonized effort for memory, and a dozen hands closed about her gently, leading her to a bench.

"Sit here, rest a while," the neighbors said. "Ah, what a beautiful rose! Never was anything so wonderful seen here in Estaban—and a holy man gave to you, *nonna?* Hush—do not try to tell us yet; rest here. Anna, run quickly, bring a mug of water."

Concetta opened her eyes and looked at the circle of kindly faces with a feeble smile. "He said to me, 'Take this to the village and tell the people the day of their deliverance is at hand,'" she murmured, as Anna thrust the mug of water toward her and a motherly hand steadied it to Concetta's lips.

The rose was still in her wrinkled fingers, and now the inhabitants of the village eyed it with reserve. Concetta sipped a little water, pushed away the mug and made another effort. "See," she said, "it is red, is it not?

"*Si, si,*" everyone agreed. "A beautiful color!"

"But first it was white," Concetta told them, "and then his fingers moved over it and it became red as . . . red as his monk's habit. And then he gave it to me, with the message. I came back as quickly as I could," she finished exhaustedly, "but you know? I cannot move as fast as the rest of you." Concetta sighed. "I did my best . . ."

"Of *course* you did!" a young woman said warmly. "And it was a wonderful message."

There was dead silence from the villagers crowded about. Then a handsome you man said flatly, "A wonderful message, indeed, Francesca—*if it be true.*"

Francesca straightened up slightly and flashed dark eyes at his warningly. "Gino—true or not, Concetta believes it, and look: there is the rose."

"Yes," everyone agreed. "That cannot be overlooked. A beautiful fresh red rose on the eve of All Saints' Day.

We must not forget that. Perhaps it is meant as a symbol of our saints? But who was the man Concetta met? A dark red monk's habit? I remember no such color in any of the nearby monasteries."

"Well," said Francesca with surprising acerbity, "why not see if he is still on the hilltop? And while you are about it, you can gather up the firewood Concetta dropped, and bring back the fine tree limb."

"Yes, yes." Gino grinned at her wickedly. "Of course, we will. Torches! It will be entirely night before we return, but the good wives will keep your suppers hot, men—and if nothing else, Concetta will have a full woodbox."

"I need nothing more than my rose," Concetta said with dignity. Pulling herself painfully from the bench, she turned toward her dismal cottage. "If only it would live forever," she murmured, and hobbled away while the villagers fell back to make a path for her.

It was a full hour before the men returned from their search of the hill. "Nothing!" Gino said to Francesca's anxious face. "Yes, there was the heap of twigs and brush and the big tree limb, as Concetta described. The men found a few other good pieces of firewood for her on the other side of the hill, too—but there was no sign of the monk, Francesca."

"Do you think he was only a devil's hallucination?" she whispered, frightened. "But—why a rose? Why not a gold piece, or an armload of firewood, enough to last through the winter?"

Gino put his arms about her comfortingly. "Yes," he said soberly, "I have thought these things, too—and I believe Concetta did meet a man in a red monk's habit, playing cards on the hilltop, who worked a miracle with a rose and promised us deliverance," his face twisted violently, "from an intolerable tyranny." His arms tightened fiercely, drawing Francesca close against him until she cried out. He let her go instantly. "Sorry, my dear one," he said absently, and turned away to clench a fist and pound it into his other palm, pacing back and forth.

"We are only peasants, perhaps," he said suddenly, "but we are *human*, as Our Lord Himself was once a human. They tell me He died on the cross to save the rest of us—but from what, Francesca? From what?"

He flung away from her, while Francesca twisted her hands together anguished, seeking words.

"They say God helps those who help themselves," Gino went on passionately, "But the Lord knows how hard we work, how diligently, how faithfully—and all for naught. Every last grain of wheat is counted, and taken away, for a vicious villain who chanced to be born in a castle instead of a manger."

"Gino, *hush!*" Francesca protested, glancing about in alarm.

"Yes," Gino agreed cynically, "Prince Prospero has spies every-where." With a snort of laughter, he turned back and caught her against him again, staring down at her intently. "I love you," he said quietly. "I've loved you since we were little children, helping our parents in the fields. There was never any other woman for me but you, 'Cesca."

"Nor any man for me but you!" she whispered, arching her back to raise her lips to his—but Gino's eyes were fixed on the small polished wooden cross hanging at the hollow of her throat.

"I believe," he said, half to himself. "I *believe* the time has come. You know why we have not married, long since?" His arms tightened gently. "We would have to have his permission. One glance at you, Francesca, and he would claim the first night, never fear!" Gino laughed shortly and kissed her lingeringly. "*Carissima*," he whispered tensely, "you may live and die unwed—for never will I permit him to have you!"

"I understand," she whispered in return, "and I am content, Gino. *Quite* content, do you hear? I will be yours—or belong to no one!"

Chapter II

IN CONCETTA'S COTTAGE, the red rose dipped and danced gracefully in the November gales that pierced the chinks in the walls, and its perfume filled the room. The villagers had gone back to their daily tasks, but the old woman sat on her stool alternately adoring the spot of glowing beauty and warming herself before a lavish fire. A criminal waste of the fine wood the men had brought back for her from their search of the hill, but old Concetta was intoxicated by her experience. The one fine tree limb that had begun the whole thing, by luring her toward the tree where the holy man could speak to her—that was reverently set aside, still dedicated to warm the Christ Child's birthday.

Meanwhile, she meant to have a good fire, to feel some semblance of the odd warmth that had touched her while she stood near the holy one in his red monk's habit, until the rose should fade—but so far, the petals were as fresh as ever. Concetta rocked back and forth, hugging herself luxuriously on her fire stool. Once in a while, she would rise painfully and hobble across to breathe deep of the scent, to place a tremulous forefinger on a petal, and the mere touch seemed to recreate the warmth within her, so that she felt almost young and gay, light-headed with joy.

In her concentration on the pleasant fire, the wonder of the rose, Concetta was oblivious of the thundering horses' hooves and the fanfare of horns outside, but the other inhabitants of Estaban were only too aware of its meaning . . .

From far down the winding road, their quicker ears had caught the first notes of the horns, approaching steadily. Within the miserable cottages, husbands looked at wives tight-lipped and grim-faced. From the pastures and byres, the younger people hastily returned to their homes, gathering together with their families. Even the children swiftly tethered their goats or raced back from the nearby woods, to the safety of *home.*

Nearer and nearer sounded the horns. Now the villagers could begin to hear the horses, the sound of carriage wheels. Then men of Estaban squared their shoulders with a deep breath, and said heavily, "What must be, must be," while their wives sought to comfort them—by a fleeting touch, an apology for a smile of encouragement, a glance of loving trust.

By ones and twos, they emerged from the cottages to stand with subservient folded arms beside their doors, while the outriders of the entourage appeared far down the dusty road. It was a glittering spectacle that approached: guards dressed in leather jerkins and chain mail, their helmets gleaming in the slanting rays of the wintry sun, with huge ebony plumes tossing in the cold wind . . . followed by the courtiers dressed in velvets and laces of silver or gold, shod in finest leather boots, with billowing cloaks and plumbed hats to keep them warm.

The guards' horses were outfitted uniformly, with black saddle cloths bearing their master's coat of arms, but the courtier's horses were gaily decked out in a fanciful array of colors that harmonized with their riders' apparel. Some of the guards carried banners; others flourished their horns and blew vigorously.

It was a brilliant show, indeed, but it brought no pleasure to the villagers, for behind it would be the coach drawn at breakneck pace by six magnificent black horses, that signified the approach of their master and epitomized the slavery of their lives. There were those who annually prayed secretly that the great coach would fail to negotiate the wicked curve in the road leading to the straightway to Estaban, that it might overturn and break the neck of its occupant, but neither God nor the Devil had so far answered their prayers.

In fact, they might better have prayed for the disablement of Price Prospero's coachman, for now, as always, his skill brought the coach swaying but safe around the curve, and with a shout of triumph, his long whip flicked forward to urge an even faster pace from the horses.

Silently, the villagers waited as the entourage came toward them—until there was a sudden faint scream of agony from one woman. *"My baby!"*

Concentrating on the riders, no one had noticed the infant crawling forward into the dirt road, where now it sat, happy cooing to itself and patting the dust! On came the outriders, with no slackening in pace, while the white-faced young husband restrained his distracted wife from rushing forward. "They will only kill both of you, Lisa."

From the opposite side of the road, Gino gauged his strength, plunged into the road, to scoop up the baby and whirl back against a hut—exactly as the guards and following courtiers poured into the tiny village square, where they formed a ring about the outer edges that at some points brought them dangerously close to the silent inhabitants. Uncontrollably, the villagers shrank back from the curvetting horses and their iron-shod hooves, while the black coach horses were pulled to a prancing, wheeling halt in the center of the square.

Two footmen in the well-known black velvet livery sprang down to seing open the carriage door and swiftly lower the folding steps. It was a beautiful carriage, of the finest construction, the latest model, the richest materials within and the most intricate decoration without. It glowed with the tiny glints of gold paint here, and richest ruby red there—a touch of sapphire blue cunningly outlining the delicate carving about the door, and a cartouche painted upon the door panel itself.

At first glance, this appeared to be a garland of twining flowers encircling the great golden initial *P* . . .but to the community of Estaban who had had all to many opportunities to examine the cartouche in detail, it was a matter of aversion.

Not flowers, but tortured, writhing, dying human figures were depicted in that garland—and to Estaban, those figures were themselves.

Looking impassively, stonily, into space, they stood now in silence while Prince Prospero stepped leisurely down from his coach and surveyed the scene with a raised eyebrow. Estaban had no need to look at him, either. They knew only too well that he was tall, slender, aristocratically handsome: dark hair, dark eyes set deep in a face on incredibly chiselled perfection, a set of the shoulders and a carriage that embodied all the arrogance of the divine right of kings.

In contrast to the extravagant costumes of his courtiers, Prince Prospero was dressed with severe restraint, and somehow that simplicity in itself turned the entourage into gaudy, tawdry, nobodies.

His Highness took two steps forward and glanced about languidly, while he stripped of the soft leather gauntlets, one finger at a time. "I see you are all here, awaiting—no doubt breathlessly—a word from me," he remarked, in casual tone. "I have come according to my custom, to thank you personally for the year's harvest . . ."

"And to make certain we've kept little enough for ourselves," Gino muttered, in voluntarily. Turning, he thrust the baby into the arms of a village woman, while there was a dismayed gasp of protest from nearby inhabitants at his words. Unobtrusively, they sidled away from Gino, until he stood alone with one powerful middle-aged man beside him.

Among the Prince's cavalcade, there was a murmur of anger and the guards' hands flew to their swords awaiting the word of command, but Prince Prospero merely studied Gino with heavy-lidded eyes and ignored the remark—superbly. ". . . and to invite you to a feast to be held in a fortnight," he went on, uninterestedly.

"When, according to your custom, the scraps from your table will be thrown to us like dogs," Gino observed, shaking off the restraining hand of the man beside him.

Again the guards muttered angrily, and began to close in, but the prince stayed them with a raised hand. "Exactly," he said with soft emphasis, staring steadily at Gino . . .and when the younger man's gaze did not falter, he went on, "But these dogs have a loud bark and show their teeth. *Why?*"

Gino squared his shoulders and faced Prospero firmly. "An old woman of the village met a holy man on the hill on the eve of All Saint's Day," he said quietly. "He spoke to her as she was gathering firewood, and made a prophecy. He gave her a rose, and bade her tell us, here in Estaban, that the day of our deliverance was at hand."

"From your tyranny," the older man added involuntarily.

There was a breathless hush over the thronged village square, while Prince Prospero contemplated the two men before him. "Then," he inquired courteously, "shouldn't you get on your knees and give thanks?" He gestured slightly with one finger, and two guards sprang forward, joined by two others from the rear, to grasp Gino and his companion, forcing them brutally to their knees.

There was another moment of silence, while the prince cocked his head on one side and pondered. "Garotte them," he said finally, with the utmost casualness and stood still, cocking his head to the other side . . . waiting.

The guards worked most efficiently. One of each pair pinioned the men's arms; the others removed leather loops joined by a bar of wood from their belts and swiftly noosed the necks of the doomed men. From the throng, Francesca broke forward to throw herself on the ground before the victims, with an arm about each. "No!" she cried, agonized, and turned imploringly to Prospero. "No, I beg you, *no!*"

Releasing the men, she swung around and crawled over the dirt to embrace Prospero's legs, wailing, "Mercy, mercy!" Bursting into wild sobs she clung frantically, while one of the guards rapidly tore her away and flung her backward onto the ground.

Leaning over, the guard slapped her full-force in the face, hissing, "How dare you touch His Highness! You filthy pig!" Straightening up, he looked to Prospero for approbation while Francesca lay moaning on the ground, but the prince merely pushed him away with a violent thrust of his riding whip that nearly overbalanced the guard.

"The girl was addressing *me,*" Prospero remarked calmly. "What's your name?"

"Francesca." She pulled herself up again, kneeling in the dirt. "Mercy, in the name of God!" she breathed.

Half-strangled, Gino's voice was hoarse with command. "Get off your knees to—him . . ."

Prospero did not even glance at him, as the guard tightened the garotte. Looking down thoughtfully at Francesca, he repeated her name, "Francesca. Hmmmmmm. And what would you ask of me?"

"Forgive them," she whispered. "Forgive them!"

"But my dear child, that isn't possible," his voice was pained, yet patient, willing to explain. "They have defied me." He pursed his lisp and found an illustration. "If my hound bites my hand after I've fed and caressed him," he said brightly, "should I allow him to go undisciplined?"

"No, but you would not *kill* him," she pleaded. "I beg you: forgive them!"

"No, of course I would not kill a valuable dog," the prince returned instantly, and looked down at her for a moment as a faint smile touched his lips. "How innocent you are!" he commented with a shrug. "But I'm disposed to temper justice with mercy. I will leave it to you, Francesca. One must die. Which one?"

She stared up at him, dumbfounded for a moment.

"No!" she whispered, burying her face in her hands. Then she looked up at him with an odd dignity. "You have not given me a choice, your Highness," she said simply. "You couldn't know—but one is my father, Ludovico, and the other is Gino," her voice sank to a whisper, "the man I love."

"Ah? A difficult decision indeed," Prince Prospero said, insolently, and was interrupted by one of the richly dressed members of his cavalcade.

"Prospero, how long do we stay in this filthy pig-wallow?" he inquired fretfully, and widened his eyes slightly at the kneeling beauty of Francesca. He came forward to stand beside the prince and murmured, "Well, old friend! You promised me entertainment; I never hoped for this. Have such eyes ever known sin?"

"I should doubt it, Alfredo," the prince mused softly and flicked a malicious glance over the smooth facade of intelligence, and good grooming, that cloaked the unique sadism of his intimate friend. "And although they will, Alfredo, they will, he promised with a broad smile of anticipation, "it will *not* be for the delectation of the Duke of Malaga."

"Spoilsport!" the Duke complained lightly, standing aside and studying the down-bent head of Francesca. "Ah, well—when you are through, there will perhaps be something left over for me?"

"Unlikely," Prospero stated, and turned back to Francesca. "Come, girl. Make the choice: one will live, one will die . . ." and as she shook her head violently and covered her face with her hands, "Or—*both will die?*"

Tortured, Francesca raised her head and looked over her shoulder in the agony of impossible decision, while the guards tightened the leather cords that thrust back the heads of Ludovico and Gino. With the moan of a dying animal,she turned again to gaze pleadingly at the prince, but before she could say anything, the deathly stillness of the air was split by an incredible scream of pain and anguish.

Prince Prospero did not take his eyes from the tormented trio before him. "Silence that," he commanded and as a guard went swiftly toward the cottage from whence had issued the scream, the prince looked implacably at Francesca. "Choose," he said in a voice of velvety softness. "Quickly, please. Which is to die?"

Again the frightful scream rent the air, as Alfredo looked thoughtfully at the girl. "Go on, make your choice," he said analytically. "I am interested to know which comes first in your heart: filial devotion—or sensual pleasure . . ."

Prospero smiled faintly. "You put it so well, old friend!" he drawled. "Choose, girl!"

Francesca opened her lips tremulously, but as both men waited with an insulting lack of interest, there was yet a third terrifying scream, piercing and shrill, dying away into a horrible bubbling gasp, while the villagers shrank slightly and clung to each other.

Prince Prospero sighed deeply. "Must I take care of everything myself?" he remarked, with the accents of a stern yet kindly paternal disciplinarian. With a slight shrug, he turned and strode toward the hut, while the company fell back to make way for him. He drew out his dagger, kicked open the door, which promptly splintered into slivers of rotten wood, and standing on the threshold, peered briefly in at the gloom until his eyes adapted to the darkness.

"Guard!" he said commandingly, but there was no immediate

answer. Glancing about, Prince Prospero discerned by the flickering flames of the dying fire that his guard was slumped against the wall, white-faced, drooling with terror. In voluntarily, his Highness recoiled slightly and directed his gaze to the point of the guard's intent stare. It seemed to focus on a heap of rags in the center of the floor.

His dagger still poised, Prospero frowned and took two steps forward, where he leaned down and inspected the rags with mild curiosity. They seemed to be alive; they trembled, and as he drew back sharply, startled at the evidence of animation, they inched and humped themselves, worm-like, across the packed dirt floor of the hovel. Before his astonished eyes, a claw-like arm thrust forth, reaching upward toward a rough plank table on which stood a cup holding a . . . could it be a flower?

Prospero peered in concentration through the fog of the room, and identified the object: a perfectly fresh, crisp-pettalled, brilliantly glowing red rose, that seemed actually to bend from its holder to the hand seeking for it . . . to nestle within the claws that drew it feebly upward to a dim whiteness that might be a face. His Highness straightened up, thrusting the dagger into its belt sheathe, and suddenly aware of the overpowering fragrance of fresh roses . . . but even as he tried to comprehend, there was a final horrifying shriek and the claws fell aside limply, releasing the rose, which dropped across Prospero's elegant leather boot.

Impatiently, he kicked it aside and bent forward to inspect the heap of rags. He found himself looking at the withered face of an old crone. She was quite definitely dead—but even as Prospero stared down at her, the lined features were mysteriously bedewed with droplets of . . . *blood.*

His Highness drew back with a shudder working its way up the entire length of his spine. Never had he been more appalled, more caught off balance. "The Red Death!" he muttered, incredulously, and backed away a few steps until the heel of his boot struck the threshold stone, when he whirled and strode across the miserable little square with an urgent gesture to the guards holding Gino and Ludovico.

Immediately the guards released the garottes and stood back

watchfully, their eyes waiting for the next command as Francesca quavered, "Your Highness . . ."

"Silence!" Prospero said shortly and stared at the men. "That old woman who was told the prophecy—who was she?"

"Concetta," Francesca told him, bewildered. "In the hut your Highness visited . . ."

"Have you touched her?" he demanded hoarsely.

Francesca shook her head. "No."

He whirled toward Gino and Ludovico. "Or either of you?" Feebly, the men shook their heads in the negative, gently touching the cruel soreness at their throats. Prospero turned to the guards. "Take these three back to the castle. They may yet provide us some entertainment there." Swivelling on his heel, he strode toward his coach with an authoritative gesture of his riding whip above his head. "To horse, friends!"

Roughly the guards pulled Francesca, Ludovico and Gino to their feet and pushed them forward toward the entourage, as the cavaliers vaulted gay and laughing into their saddles, heedless of the wickedly kicking horse-hooves that threatened the villagers huddling frantically beside their cottages. Prince Prospero stepped rapidly into his coach, signalled the footmen to fold up the steps and close the door, and as they sprang up to their places on the vehicle, he leaned from the window and caught the eye of the captain of the guards.

"Yes, your Highness?" The man leaped forward eagerly.

"Burn this village to the ground," Prince Prospero said with awful clarity, and sank back into the coach, slamming closed the window and barking, "Forward, with all speed!" The coachman flashed his whip over the horses, skillfully manoeuvring them to and fro in the tiny village square of Estaban, while the inhabitants stood bewildered and incredulous, looking at each other and murmuring, "What did he say? No, it must be a mistake!"

Gino broke from the guards and leaped for the carriage, smashing his fist through the side window. "Why do you burn the homes?" he cried. "Winter comes! So we are less than dogs to you—but even so if we die, where is your harvest?"

Prospero's riding crop slashed across his face brutally, and as

Gino cried out sharply and threw up one arm to protect himself, the prince pried his other hand loose from the coach. Gino fell backward into the road, and Prospero's voice remarked sardonically, "*This* is your day of deliverance! *On,* driver, and make haste!"

Instinctively, Gino rolled aside from the thundering hooves of the black horses and the iron-bound carriage wheels, as the coachman achieved the turn and with a triumphant cry, "Holá!" had stung the black horses into a mad spring forward. As the carriage bowled swiftly away from the village square, the courtiers raced after it with an equal chorus of shouts, waving their arms, their plumed hats, the banners.

In a split second, the square was empty but for the horse droppings, the churned sod where the steeds had pawed the earth, and the blank-faced guards swiftly setting about their task. "You take that side; I'll do this one," a guard directed tersely, and as the villagers milled about, confused and disoriented, he darted into a cottage and returned with a burning twig from the hearth fire. Casually he reached up to hold it to the thatch until the flames caught avidly and raced upward to the ridge pole.

Holding out the burning twig, he ignited the bits of wood the other guards had found and turned to the next hovel, where a peasant woman hysterically flew at him with extended fingernails. Momentarily, the guard fended her off while he set his torch to her thatched roof, until her nails drew a line of blood down his cheek. With a muttered oath, he threw her away from him. "Hellcat!" he said, furiously, confirming the blood with a glance at his hand. "Here's a passport for you!"

Deliberately, he set his flaming torch to her hair, her shawl, and as the flames engulfed her shrieking form, he pushed her aside with a telling thrust to the stomach and went swiftly on to the next cottage—and so on, and on, until at the far end of the square he faced the other guards.

"We've got all of them," one man panted, mopping his forehead and looking about anxiously. "We'd better get out of here!"

The villagers were clustered screaming and weeping in the middle of the square. Occasionally someone would make a valiant effort to enter one or another of the burning cottages in search of some private treasure, only to be beaten back by the flames.

"What about *them?*" one of the guards inquired, jerking a thumb at the populace. "Were we supposed to get rid of them, too?"

"He didn't say," the first guard frowned, undecidedly, and put a reminiscent hand to his bleeding cheek with a curse. *"Sapristi! She fought like a tigress!"*

"You'll be marked for life, Josef," another guard said slyly, "and all the better for the rest of us, if your 'beauty' is spoiled, eh?"

There was an echoing shout of mirth from the others, while Josef stood scowling, half-flattered at the envy among his fellows.

"Did he *say* to kill people?" Guglielmo asked, literally.

The guards looked at each other. "No. He said burn the village to the ground."

Guglielmo shrugged and turned toward the castle road. "We've done it," he stated with finality—and halfway across the square, suddenly picked up his heels and began running for his life.

Behind him the other guards hesitated briefly, but as two cottages on opposite sides of the tiny square broke apart and spewed a fountain of flaming rubble across the dirt and cobblestones, the also took to their heels, leaping and dodging the fires and brutally shoving the villagers out of their way. On the outskirts of the holocaust, they paused for breath, wiping their foreheads on their jerkins, and taking a final critical look at their handiwork.

"It's all right, they told each other with satisfaction. "A good job—nothing overlooked. Eh, there should be an extra cup of wine for all of us tonight! Turning away, they swaggered off to their horses and swung into the saddles.

"What about *them?*" Guglielmo inquired, jerking a thumb toward Gino, Ludovico and Francesca, tightly bound and tethered to a tree.

"Well, *what* about them?" Bertrand returned, dismounting with a sigh. "He said: bring them up to the castle."

"How?" Guglielmo asked with great simplicity. "Do we carry 'em on our horses . . . or make 'em walk . . .or drag 'em?"

"Put a filthy peasant pig on *my* horse? Josef said. "Not on your life!"

Bertrand considered. "He said bring them to the castle where they might afford some entertainment," he remembered. "Better not to drag 'em. He won't like it if they arrive damaged."

"All right," Guglielmo agreed. "They walk . . . but they'll have to be quick about it, because we are already miles behind the rest of them. I must say, I'd almost rather carry 'em on our saddles. I don't like to get so far away from His highness . . . no knowing what he mightn't decide to do when he gets back to the castle. Leave us to spend the night outside, most likely, if he's in one of his tantrums. . ."

"Guglielmo's made a very good point there," Louis observed. All the guards looked at each other undecidedly; even Josef was half-convinced, until Bertrand who had untied the victims from their tree said over his shoulder, "An excellent point—if you can stand the smell!" His nose wrinkled with disgust. "Faugh! They must live on garlic!"

"That settles it," said Josef, and spurred forward as swiftly as possible. "I'll go on and try to catch up; Louis come with me—your mount's as fast as mine. If we can make it in time, we'll keep the bridge open for you."

In a swirl of dust the two guards were gone, while Guglielmo looked after them with disfavor. "If that isn't *exactly* like Josef," he observed, as Bertrand swung into his own saddle. "Always an unanswerable reason for getting out of anything unpleasant!"

"Oh, *yes,*" Bertrand concurred, resignedly, but what can you do? He's a Medici bastard, and you can't deny he's got plenty of old Alessandro's wits! Who was it got us the extra measures of wine . . . and a ducat apiece for getting rid of those Venetians who were interfering with the ships from Cyprus?"

Guglielmo grinned. "I know, and I like him as well as you do," he remarked. "The guard room's a different place since he came, and I don't deny he handles himself well! Doesn't give himself any airs, doesn't question your authority as captain, never a word of criticism of you, Bertrand! Pulls his weight in any fight, takes your orders. . .the only trouble," Guglielmo grinned again, "You're too slow about giving 'em!"

Bertrand laughed ruefully, shaking his head. "You mean, he thinks faster than I do—and he's quietly vanished before I can *give* the order. Oh, well," he said philosophically, "what you say is all true, but I'd as soon have him beside me in a fight than any man I could name—no offence, Guglielmo! He's got a skill with that sword, and you'll notice he never shirks a *real* duty."

"Such as finding enough wenches for all of us," Guglielmo remarked, slyly. "*Holá*, you there, you peasant pigs—get going!" With the flat of his sword, he swung downward across the men's posteriors, driving them forward at a faster pace while Francesca tried for a final look at the burning village as they rounded the curve in the road. Her eyes blinded with tears, she stumbled and fell in the dust like a driven animal. Gino's strong arm pulled her to her feet.

"Courage, my darling!" he muttered. "It is all in the hands of God, and surely He will not desert us!"

"But it is not only for ourselves, but for all the people in Esteban," she caught her breath and sobbed uncontrollably. "Oh, Gino, did you see! Everything gone, nothing left—only our friends, praying on their knees under the trees. What will happen to them, what *can* happen to them?"

"Hush, dearest one!" he said softly, steadying her swaying form as best he could in his own exhaustion. "Now is not the moment to think of what is behind and gone, but to ask His strength for whatever lies ahead."

Wearily, Francesca put one hand over the wooden cross at her neck and clutched convulsively. "Yes of course you are right, my love," she murmured. "If His Son could endure, so can we, but," she trembled with sudden sobs, "Gino, I'm—*frightened* . . ."

"Move along, move along!" Bertrand's sword prodded them firmly, and as the three of them made an effort to hasten out of reach of that painful *spank*, Bertrand's eyes peered keenly up the winding road toward the castle. There were still numerous curves to traverse, but from this particular spot he could see the entrance gate, the drawbridge, the portcullis. "It's all right so far," he remarked. "Everything open . . ."

Guglielmo squinted reflectively, gauging the well-known road against the slow pace of their captives. "I think we'll make it," he said. "Look—that spurt of dust, there; that must be Josef and Louis, already at the last curve behind the rest of them."

"Yes, they'll catch up! Bertrand agreed with a sigh of relief. "If only these pigs would move faster . . ."

Guglielmo surveyed the stumbling figures plodding along in the dust. "Better not push 'em any more," he advised, authoritatively. "Have to let 'em make their own pace now; it's steep, and the girl's ready to drop as it is."

Bertrand studied Francesca's exhausted figure, supported by Ludovico and Gina, and moving forward one step at a time like an automaton. "You're right," he agreed fretfully. It's probably the girl he wants. Better not let her arrive in a faint . . ."

"I *said* we should have tied them on the backs of our saddles," Guglielmo remarked philosophically. "We'd have there by now, if we had."

"You didn't smell 'em," Bertrand returned flatly. "Even *behind* you, after four miles, you wouldn't fancy your dinner tonight, believe me . . ."

Chapter III

WITHIN THE CAREENING COACH leading the cavalcade, Prince Prospero sat back, white-faced and intent, clinging to the side strap to hold himself in his sear. Behind him thundered the horses of his courtiers, with the Duke of Malaga in the forefront, but in his concentration of thought, Prospero was scarcely aware of the gay horns, the joyous cries from the riders behind him.

"The Red Death?" he thought, and frowned slightly. Perhaps not, after all, and he'd only been panicked by a trivial peasant village incident. He scowled involuntarily at the possibility, even in his own mind, of less-than-bravery. Still best not to take any chances, and he had shown his inherited leadership in his command to burn Estaban to the ground. Glancing idly from the coach window as they swung around a curve, Prospero could see the leaping flames from the village below. His dark eyes observed without interest. Naturally, there would be flames. He had commanded it, and thus it would be without question.

Thoughtfully, he pursed his lips and considered once more. No longer any real danger, if any had indeed ever existed—but better to be safe than sorry. A pity this should have occurred n Estaban, where the villagers were diligent in making the most of the fields. The castle would miss that harvest next year. He sighed, exasperated, but after reflection, Prospero was able to commend his forthright handling of the situation. His overseers would simply have to beat the peasants on the rest of his holdings into working harder, and in a year or two, Estaban could be re-established. Unquestionably, there'd be plenty of peasants anxious to have the use of the till-age, where pasturage was lush, fattening animals with practically no effort; fields completely cleared of stones and roots, producing lavish crops for a minimum of work.

Prince Prospero relaxed in the corner of his coach and abandoned consideration of Estaban. Now he was dimly aware of the gaiety among the companions on the road behind him and thought, instead, of the revelry ahead. It was a matter of record, unquestioned, accepted, taken for granted, that anyone so fortunate as to be a guest of Prince Prospero's might be certain of the finest, most unique, entertainment in the world.

Tonight's schedule was planned; what of the morrow? A sudden tiny smile played about Prospero's mouth, spreading outward and upward to lend a keen glint to the bored dark eyes. Almost, one might have said that Prince Prospero had become alert, that he had had an idea of positive excitement . . .

Grasping the coach strap firmly, he stared with narrowed eyes into space, and thought furiously. Once more he was oblivious to the fanfare and hullabaloo behind him, until the coach swerved around in a long graceful sweep and the horses were thundering across the iron-strapped wooden planks of the drawbridge. From each cranny and corner of the castle courtyard dashed servants, springing to their appointed tasks of leaping to halt the foam-flecked wild-eyed horses of the carriage . . . to hold open doors, to lead away the steed of Prince Prospero's entourage as soon as they had dismounted.

The carriage footmen had tumbled to the ground and raced to open the door, let down the steps—but for a full minute, His Highness did not emerge. While the stableboys clung full force to the carriage horses, and the courtyard gradually became crowded with more and more of the gay courtiers and guests, swinging down from their horses and milling about, one footman dared to clear a throat, to essay a cautious sidewise peek into the coach. "yes, yeessss!" he drawled softly to himself. "The very thing!" With a chuckle, he pulled himself leisurely forward and emerged swiftly, but without panic, from the carriage. Momentarily he paused again, looking absently into space, while the footmen rapidly closed up the carriage and it was led away to the coach-house. Unobtrusively, half a dozen servants hovered within earshot, waiting . . . No knowing *what* his Highness might be contemplating, but woe betide the whole staff if the exact right minion were not at hand when Prince Prosper chose to speak!

"Couriers," said Prospero finally, fingering his beard thoughtfully. A page raced instantly toward the stables while a man at the back of the group turned and sauntered away; he was the head cook, and while life might grow hectic in the kitchens later on, at the moment there was no need for him in the courtyard. The steward would tell him in due course how many guests were in the castle, and meanwhile Arturo might as well return to his siesta. There would be still an hour before he need rouse himself to supervise the forthcoming banquet, and personally Arturo *loathed* the stench of horses.

As he passed tranquilly into the corridor leading to the kitchens, mounted horsemen raced from the stables, to bring their steeds to a prancing standstill at a respectful distance from the Prince, who was now issuing orders crisp as a general deploying forces before a battle.

"To the castle of the Duke of Verga—to Florence and Signor Lampredi," said Prospero, stabbing a finger at one after another of the couriers. "You—to Verone, and you, to Milan . . ." As he paused briefly, thinking hard, Josef and Louis dashed into the courtyard and drew their horses to a stop. Prince Prospero glanced at them vaguely. "Well?"

The guards drew themselves erect on their horses and Josef said, "Your orders have been carried out, Your Highness. The village of Estaban has been burned to the ground, and Bertrand and Guglielmo bring the three peasants for your entertainment."

"Peasants?" Prospero repeated, and thought for a moment.

"Oh—*peasants*, of course!" He snapped a finger gently and a servant ran forward. "The girl: give her a bath. The men: into the lower dungeon." He snapped the finger again and the servant murmured, "Yes, *Excellenzia!"* and vanished into the background.

"Josef!" said Prospero with a brilliant smile, as if this were the one face on earth he wished to see.

"Yes, your Highness!"

"To Favenna, and," Prospero sketched a wink, "you-know-who?"

"*Certainly,* your Highness!"

Prospero's heavy-lidded glance flicked over the handsome young guard. "But you return *at once,"* he remarked softly, "escorting Donna Esterra in complete safety. That is understood?"

"Yes, your Highness," Josef's voice was suavely amazed at the implication of any other possibility!

Prospero smiled sardonically, and turned to the waiting courtiers. "Tell my friends they must come without delay," he said, "and *to avoid the village of Estaban!* On your way, with all speed!"

"Si, subito, Excellenzia! Andiamo! Holá, clear the way there . . ." The couriers spurred their horses and dashed forth across the bridge, to separate like wheat grains in the wind as each rider took a different road and vanished in a cloud of dust.

Prince Prospero turned and crossed the courtyard to the great doors of the castle, followed by the laughing guests and courtiers. Simultaneously, the keeper of the bridge bent to the wheel beginning to draw it up, until Louis sprang forward and hissed, "Delay a little man!"

"Eh?" the bridge guard straightened up and looked stupidly at Louis, who grasped his arm firmly.

"Bertrand and Guglielmo," he muttered, "bringing those three peasants! We came ahead, Josef and I, to warn you: keep the bridge open for a bit." He fixed the bridge guard with a steely glance and added, "If you raise the bridge now, you'll only have to lower it again in a short while, Luigi!"

"Eh, I don't like this," Luigi said uneasily. "You know His Highness's strict orders . . ."

"And also how much effort it takes to raise and lower the

bridge," Louis countered. "Listen, they cannot be too far away by now; let me go onto the bridge and take a look?"

Anxiously Luigi looked back over his shoulder, but by now the glittering company had passed into the great hall of the castle and the doors were closed. "If he should happen to see the bridge still open?" he debated.

"He will not!" Louis glanced about hastily and sighed with relief to find no one within earshot. "You go too far, Louis! One day . . ." he shook his head solemnly and drew a finger across his throat graphically.

"Morbleu!" Louis swore vehemently. "Do you then *wish* to raise—*and* lower—the bridge in the space of two breaths? Without waiting for an answer, he strode out to the edge of the drawbridge and peered down the road toward the defunct village. Striding quickly back, he called, "I can see them! They're at the final curve. If you raise now, you'll only just have got it up as they arrive . . ."

Luigi looked at the heavy wheel and wavered. "But what shall I say if his Highness *does* notice the bridge is down when he is within?" he asked shakily. "I shall be whipped!"

"Oh, say anything!" Louis returned impatiently. "Say the cords slipped slightly . . . Go on, bend over and pretend to be fixing the chair. Only a few minutes, Man!" He strode back across the bridge and peered down the road again, to call back encouragingly, "They are nearly here. Another few paces . . ."

To Guglielmo and Bertrand, the figure waving vigorously at the edge of the open bridge was a welcome sight. "Good old Louis!" Bertrand heaved a sigh of relief. "I knew he would not forget! Come on, you pigs—move! With the flat of his sword he struck viciously at Gino and Ludovico, who groaned involuntarily while Francesca slumped to the ground between them.

"I *told* you not to be hasty!" Guglielmo remarked with deep censure. "Now look what you've done! They'll have to get her up on her feet and moving again—and heaven knows how long they'll take. When we were so nearly there, too!"

"Oh, all right, sorry," Bertrand returned sulkily, as the men pulled Francesca erect with their final strength and the trio patiently plodded forward again. "I'll ride ahead," he announced, brightening suddenly. "Once I am on the bridge, too, it will surely stay open for you." Spurring his horse forward, Bertrand quickly gained the entrance to the castle, where he sat proudly on his horse and engaged in converse with Louis in the exact center of the bridge.

Guglielmo could recognize and approve these masterly delaying tactics, but after Bertrand's final *swat* with his sword, the three peasants were moving more and more slowly. With sudden decision, Guglielmo pulled his horse alongside, and said, "Girl! Put your foot into the stirrup and give me your hand. You, push her up!" Dully Gino and Ludovico obeyed, and Francesca lay half-collapsed across Guglielmo's knees. "Now—come on!" he said, and wrinkled his nose involuntarily. "Jesù, Bertrand was right! Ugh, the smell. Have they never heard of water!"

Without the weight of Francesca between them, Gino and Ludovico did progress a bit more quickly, while Louis and Bertrand continued the delaying tactics in the center of the drawbridge. Luigi was shivering with fright and about to abandon the whole thing, when a servant darted out from the castle and demanded imperiously, "*Where* are those peasants his Highness ordered?"

"Coming, coming," Luigi said hastily, and with a sigh of relief observed the sad procession just stepping onto the bridge. "Will you hurry up!" he cried angrily. "The bridge must be closed!"

Bending to his wheel, he strained to his task, while Louis, Bertrand and Guglielmo thundered into the courtyard leaving Gino and Ludovico stranded on the rising bridge which, in its passing, unbalanced them so they tumbled into an exhausted heap on the cobblestones. "If you want 'em, move 'em away," Luigi advised. "They are lying right across the gate."

Swiftly, Bertrand and Louis dismounted and dragged the two men aside, just as the portcullis sank its fangs into its slots and the great bridge closed beyond it. "The men into the lower dungeon, but not harmed," the servant reported. "The girl comes with me."

"Good," said Guglielmo, releasing his grasp on Francesca's hand so that she slipped backward into a heap on the stone blocks and lay gasping for breath.

"Up! said the servant distainfully, while Guglielmo turned his horse toward the barracks, Francesca scrambled to her feet as quickly as possible, but Gino and Ludovico were already lost to her, being hustled along by Bertrand and Louis. Even as she tried to call after them, they had vanished through the grilled doorway.

With a whimper, Francesca slumped sideways against the servant, who thrust her erect and said, "Ugh! Don't touch me! Come on, and be quick about it—*that* way!" He pointed a contemptuous forefinger to the other side of the courtyard. "Through the scullery, and what his Highness with *you* is more than *I* can tell," the man grumbled, as Francesca stumbled forward.

Dimly, she heard the heavy iron door swing shut behind her with ominous finality. Automatically, she plodded up what seemed an endless flight of worn stone steps, and found herself directed into a large bedchamber, facing three hard-eyed women. "Here she is, and rather you than I!" said the servant, light-heartedly, and slammed the door behind her.

Francesca looked dully at the cold faces. "Please . . ." she whispered, and felt herself crumpling to nothing . . .

Chapter IV

SHE CAME ALIVE SLOWLY, hearing the sound of water, the voices of women cackling in an exchange of banter, and leisurely footsteps passing back and forth about her. Francesca lay still as a hunted animal and fought wildly for strength. If only her heart would stop pounding so desperately, if only she could think, if only she knew the fate that lay ahead!

Very, very cautiously, she peeked through her eye-lashes and assessed the situation. Directly before her was a huge tin tub, from which steam arose in clouds as the servants pouring into it successive pots of hot water. Involuntarily, Francesca opened her eyes wide; did they mean to boil her?

"She's alive," one woman observed impersonally. "You, Maria; get her on her feet and out of those rags. Lucia, bring cold water."

With a deep sigh of disgust, Maria approached and stood over Francesca, holding out a tentative hand. "Will you rise, milady?" she asked impassively, as Francesca merely lay still upon the floor and stared at the woman. "if you *please,* milady," Maria added with mock sweetness—and reached down to yank Francesca erect with a ruthless had. "You will wash."

"In my own time," Francesca said, stepping back two paces and raising her chin, firmly.

"The Prince says *now* is the time," Lucia said calmly and advanced with determination.

Francesca retreated another two paces and raised her chin even more haughtily. "I will do *nothing* until I know about Gino and my father."

"Listen to her!" Lucia snorted, while Maria closed in from the rear. "You will do exactly as you're told, my fine lady! Come on—off with those indecent rags." Francesca's dark eyes blazed with fury as Maria's strong arm pushed her forward. She fell on Lucia with nails out-stretched. "Ayeeee!" Lucia squealed, in alarm, but she was no match for the three serving women. Between them, her ragged dress was ruthlessly ripped away until she stood naked. Laughing coarsely, they gripped her and tumbled her headfirst into the tub, ducking back from the splashing sheets of hot water sprayed upward. Automatically, Francesca pulled herself right side up, sputtering, with one hand on the edge of the tub and the other brushing the wet hair from her eyes.

As she opened her mouth and tried to stand up, to continue the battle, she was aware of the three servants falling back respectfully and heard a ringing laugh from the door. She turned quickly to see Prince Prospero with a handsome woman in court dress beside him. His face brimmed with amusement, as Francesca tried to cover herself with her hands and nearly slid own into the tub once more.

"Modesty but no humility, eh, Juliana?" Prospero remarked, with a chuckle.

"As you say, your Highness," Juliana murmured subserviently, appraising Francesca's youth and beauty with narrowed eyes, while Prospero sauntered forward.

"My father and Gino?" Francesca demanded. "Where are they?"

"Why do you hide yourself? Prospero asked, gently.

"It's not right that you should look at me."

"You wear a Cross about your neck. It is only a decoration, or are you a true Christian believer?"

"Yes," she said. "I believe. Most truly!"

He pursed his lips. "Then I'd like you to remove it and never wear it within this castle again." He held out his hand authoritatively, averting his head. Francesca hesitated and he made in impatient gesture with his hand. Slowly she removed the Cross and dropped it into his hand, sinking low into the tub to hide herself, as he walked to the night table beside the bed and tossed the Cross on the polished top without a glance.

"Is this peasant to use my room for her baths?" Juliana asked involuntarily.

"We'll find another room for you," Prospero shrugged. Meanwhile, you'll see that the lady Francesca is dressed in one of your finest gowns. Later you will instruct her in the ways of the Court." Indolently, he went toward the door while Juliana flushed angrily and bit her lips at his reproof.

"Please!" Francesca cried strongly from her tub. "My father?"

His Highness paused at the door without turning, "Oh, yes," he said pleasantly. "You father and your lover are quartered in a warm, safe place. Very safe and extremely warm, He chuckled and disappeared into the corridor.

Juliana closed the door behind him softly and came toward Francesca. "You may have impressed the Prince with all this modesty and no humility," she stated, "but you can count on no help from me."

"You will do as he told you," Francesca countered.

Juliana studied her in silence. "Yes," she agreed after a moment. "As we all must do."

"*I* will do whatever I must to save my men," Francesca said defiantly, "but if they are killed I shall die and so will Prince Prospero!"

Juliana's face twisted sardonically as she signalled the servants to leave. "Once—a time ago," she told Francesca evenly, "*I,* too, thought such brave and foolish thoughts."

"When the time comes, *I* won't lose my courage."

"There are things in this castle far beyond anything you can imagine," Juliana said, not unkindly, and shook her head at the younger girl with a sad half-smile. "When the time comes to face them, your courage will be of little avail."

Francesca gripped the edge of the tub convulsively, her eyes staring up at Juliana. Suddenly there were tinkling chimes and Juliana turned quickly to peer at the delicate French clock on the night stand. "Later than I realized," she muttered and was galvanized into activity. "Come, girl, make haste. We must hurry. No, don't protest! You'll only pay higher in the end."

Rapidly Juliana went to the huge armoire and threw back the doors, searching among the beautiful gowns hanging within and drawing out a shimmering golden robe. "See," she said, clutching the dress against her, "my finest dress!" Turning toward Francesca, she smiled drily. "Not because Prospero commands me, my dear—but because after all and even though you will now supplant me, you touch my heart, you foolish innocent."

Under the spell of Juliana's energy, Francesca was hypnotized into clambering awkwardly out of the tub, to dry herself on the cloths warming before the fire, and to insert herself into the lovely golden gown. Breathlessly, the servants returned at Juliana's summons, to dress Francesca's hair modishly, to touch salve to her lips and perfume ointment between her breasts and behind her ears, while Juliana hovered by, urging haste and giving directions.

When at last Francesca stood up and surveyed herself in the long dressing mirror, she caught her breath and turned impulsively to Juliana. "Whatever lies ahead for me, I thank you for your courtesy and help, milady!"

Juliana eyed her inscrutably. "No thanks are due to me, milady—for perhaps I help myself in helping you. We shall see." Turning to the door, she motioned Francesca to follow. "The revels have started already, but we will hope to arrive before his Highness notices our absence . . . that is," as Francesca stumbled badly in the unaccustomed court shoes, "if you do not fall down the stairs and break you neck! For heaven's sake, hold *up* the shirt and take *small* steps."

"I wish I had had more time to practice," Francesca said breathlessly, watching Juliana and trying her best to emulate the other woman's graceful swimming-forward motions.

"There will be more than enough time for practice," Juliana replied with finality. "Far more time than you will care to think on . . ."

From far below, seeping up the curving stone staircase, Francesca could hear intermittent strains of music and high-pitched laughter. For a moment, she shrank back in terror. Then as Juliana set her hand gracefully upon the carved handrail, and went elegantly downward with her skirt raised precisely to miss contact with the steps, Francesca took a deep breath. "It all depends on me, I must not lose faith, I must not lose courage. I must not fear or I may ruin all," she told herself. "Dear Lord, I pray you help me!"

Steadily she went forward and placed her hand upon the handrail, set her foot on the first step of the staircase . . .

In the great hall of the castle, already a number of Prince Prospero's friends summoned by the couriers had arrived and were greeting each other with pleasure. Alfredo, Duke of Malaga, was jovially sipping his wine and exchanging indecent remarks with a fading harlot, Anna-Marie, sitting next to him. Signor Lampredi was lolling nervously in his chair, holding the hand of his dear friend Clistor: a blond, curly-haired, sleepy-eyed young man.

"I wonder what scheme Prospero has in mind for us this time," Alfredo said, idly. "Something famous, I'll be bound."

"As always," Lampredi agreed. "Ah, more guests! Signor Veronese . . ."

"And the Escobar with him," Clister added disdainfully. "Dreadful woman!"

Lampredi stroked his hand gently. "Shhh, we can't all be as beautiful as you, dear boy."

The newcomers were a grotesque pair, the man obese and sinister with small sly eyes buried in folds of flesh, and the woman sweeping along beside him in complete confidence that she was the most beautiful desirable woman in the world. Her gown was designed to permit everyone to understand this confidence. They exchanged hearty greetings with the earlier guests, accepted their cups of wine and sank into chairs, where they continued a conversation already begun. Veronese took a deep gulp of his wine, and said, "I was about to speak of the anatomy of terror . . ."

As the others leaned forward attentively, Prospero's voice spoke behind them. "And what would you know of it? Your senses are much to blunt." The Prince came toward them and sat down in the great carved chair, holding up one hand. "What is terror? Listen!"

Spellbound, the room was silent while the ticking of a clock could be heard.

"That is to awaken and hear the passing of time," Prospero said, "Or—is it the failing beat of your own heart? Or the footsteps of someone who, just a moment before, was in your room?" The clock struck suddenly, musically, majestically, in deep ringing tones. Anna-Marie started and shivered involuntarily, but the mood was broken and everyone laughed nervously. "Let's not dwell on terror," Prospero said lightly,rising from his chair and gesturing slowly and gracefully with his wine goblet. "The first of my entertainments for you: the dancers Hop-Toad and Esmeralda."

All heads turned toward the center of the great hall. From the opposite side appeared a kind of large sedan chair, its curtains drawn, its poles carried by four servants. They came forward and carefully lowered the chair to the floor. Two footmen positioned themselves on either side, holding branched candelabra whose candlelight was directed on the curtains by means of shining reflectors.

Now the curtains parted to reveal a tiny stage, complete with chairs and scenery to scale . . . and a tableau that drew a chorus of delighted "Oh" and "Ah!" from the guests.

Esmeralda was a midget of perfect and exquisite proportions. She stood poised in the classic ballet position, her hand resting lightly upon a grayhound standing nearly immobile beside her, while Prospero's court jester, Hop-Toad, knelt at her feet. Ungainly and deformed as he was, the dwarf's suit of powder blue velvet made him seem a graceful and essential completion of the charming scene.

For a second the tableau held motionless, then a bell tinkled, the music began softly, and the tiny ballerina came to life, escorted off the stage to the ballroom floor by the gallant Hop-Toad, and fol-lowed by the grayhound who reseated itself, yawning with boredom but trained for the dance performance. Esmeralda curtsied formally to the guests, while Hop-Toad backed away from her like a courtier retreating from a queen . . . and as he stood in the shadows at the edge of the ballroom, it was obvious from the sparkle of his eyes that to Hop-toad, the tiny woman was in very truth the queen of his humble heart. His poor, deformed face was lit as though by inner candlelight, his eyes following every motion, every gesture, with adoration.

It was an enchanting performance! Esmeralda seemed no more than a pretty butterfly beside the sleek grayhound. Her steps were wistful, her motions tender, while a small smile flickered about her lips. She caressed the dog's head, and drew an affectionate motion from the grayhound, who nevertheless was well-trained and remained immobile as she danced away once more.

Anna-Marie clapped her hands in delight, while Alfredo's eyes narrowed with sudden interest. Prince Prospero moved silently alongside the Duke and began to sit down—and miraculously where there was no chair a moment before, *now* a footman produced one. Prospero simply lowered himself, without a glance; of course there would be a chair whisked beneath him wherever he chose to sit. He expected nothing less.

"Wherever did you find her?" Alfredo asked, leaning forward to set his wine glass on the floor at his feet without taking his eyes from Esmeralda.

"A pretty toy, isn't she?" Prospero remarked, noting the glitter in his friend's eyes.

"Delightful! I wonder . . ."

"I'm sure you do," Prospero murmured archly. "I'm sure you wonder about every female in my household. Every one that has the appearance of innocence,"

"You seem to take pleasure in corrupting it."

"Not corrupting, Alfredo! Prospero protested gently. "Instructing! Teach the virgin that her virginity is loathsome, convince the pious man his virtues are vain and therefore sinful, accuse the martyr of self-pity."

Alfredo's eyes studied the Prince and he grinned evilly, but before he could say anything, Esmeralda's tiny foot upset his wine glass, sending the red liquid across his ankle.

Caught up in her performance, she had moved closer and closer to the circle of spectators . . . and of course there should *not* have been a wine glass on the floor. She was scarcely aware when her foot skimmed outward and just touched the delicate crystal; she had almost moved on in her dance when Alfredo turned sharply from his conversation with the Prince. With a muffled curse, he lashed out instinctively . . . not a hard blow, merely the reprimand one might give to a dog, but tiny as she was, Esmeralda stumbled and fell.

She sprawled upon the floor, her dignity shattered and tears welling in her eyes, her dainty dance brought to a horrible conclusion of humiliation. In the shadows at the side of the floor, Hop-Toad's eyes flashed with hatred and instinctively his hand flew to the poignard at his side. Then his lips firmed craftily; this was not a time to fight. Quickly, he went forward to lift Esmeralda to her feet, while Alfredo was fussing over his wine-stained ankle.

"Clumsy wench! If she were full size, she'd drown us all in wine," he grumbled, swabbing viciously with a table napkin.

The other guest were either calm or faintly amused at his annoyance. No one looked at the dwarf and the midget dancer who stood hesitantly before Prince Prospero until he made a small gesture of dismissal. Then Hop-Toad solicitously led Esmeralda away to the shadows beyond the ballroom floor, while Prospero's eyes followed them appraisingly. When they had disappeared he rose from his seat and said, "My first novelty seems to have failed."

With a shrug, he went on, "Tomorrow at twelve midnight we shall have a masquerade. The wardrobes of the castle are yours to use." He took a sip of his wine, and with the utmost deliberation uptilted the glass, pouring the rest of the red liquid across Alfredo's white satin breeches. There was a delighted burst of laughter as the Duke's eyes met Prospero's in fury, and he sprang to his feet.

"You go too far," he hissed. "I'm not without influence and power."

"Against the Red Death?" Prospero inquired softly.

There was instantaneous silence and everyone looked about fearfully, while the Prince went on, "It came to the village of Estaban. Already it lays waste to the countryside. Count yourselves fortunate to be in this castle and under the protection of the Prince Prospero!"

Turning away, he paused, concentrating on the great staircase behind the guests, while they were eagerly resuming their conversations and agreeing that one could not be safer than *here*. Only the Prince had seen Francesca, standing hesitant and evidently holding tight to her courage at sight of the magnificent pageantry spread before her, smiling faintly at the expression in Prospero's eyes. Gently she nudged Francesca forward. "Go on!"

Never taking his eyes from Francesca, Prospero moved toward her through the revellers like a moth drawn by a candle, shaking aside the guests who caught at his sleeve, sought to detain him for a word of gossip, until his preoccupation struck through the wine-fuddled brains. "Where's he going?" they asked each other, and turned unsteadily to follow his progress. Gradually, the room fell silent, the musicians stopped playing and Prince Prospero was at the foot of the staircase looking up . . .

As though hypnotized, Francesca straightened her shoulders and moved with graceful dignity down the final steps to lay her hand graciously in his. Prospero bowed as though she were the finest of great ladies and drew her forward to face the rest of the guests. "The lady Francesca," he stated with no further introduction. "Now continue your revels. Act according to your natures!"

Placing Francesca's hand within his arm, he moved slowly back to the central chairs, and with his other hand pointed at random—to Veronese. "You!" he said casually. "You, Veronese, who do little more than eat and swill, and dream of other things. How like a pig you are. Be one of them!"

Under the Prince's hypnotic will-power, Veronese laughed boisterously and proceeded to get down on all fours, waddling about and grunting like a pig, while gales of laughter swept over the room. Lampredi giggled loudest of all, until Prospero's eyes narrowed thoughtfully. His commanding voice cut across the din with the ease of a hot knife through butter.

"You Lampredi—you laugh at this poor pig? While you are small and insignificant, no more than a worm! Can you be a worm, Lampredi?"

"Of course!" Lampredi shouted, caught up in the madness. "Watch me!" He flopped down on his belly set his hands behind his back and wriggled grotesquely across the floor, while the laughter grew more and more frenzied.

Prospero's eyes lighted next on Signora Escobar, who magnificent breast heaved dangerously and whose laughter was the loudest and most raucous of all. "Hear how she laughs! he cried. "It's like nothing so much as the bray of a jackass! Be one then!"

Obediently, the woman set her hands on either side of her head, waggling them in a semblance of long ears, and brayed her horrible laughter. Drunkenly, she fell to hands and knees and thew back her head in the pose of a braying ass, while Prospero smiled gently. A line of the most refined and depraved cruelty etched itself about his mouth, stretching out and up to the corners of his eyes, as he surveyed his guest, while Francesca turned away her head in shame and nausea at the indignities so willingly embraced by the others. The Prince was too intent on his game of degradation to notice her reaction. "Someone must ride that jackass to market," he suggested.

"Me . . . me!" Clistor squealed, and forthwith straddled the woman, slapping her generous rump and kicking his heels into her thighs like a peasant trying to get some speed out of his donkey. "Hey, there, get going! Show a little life!"

"The rest of you," said Prospero, calmly, "show me the lives and loves of the animals! Use your imaginations . . . and a prize for the most realistic!"

Instantly, the entire throng seemingly went mad and abandoned itself to barnyard representations. Everyone knew that "a prize" from Prospero would be well worth having! It might be anything from a purse of gold ducats to an immensely valuable jewel that would automatically raise a whore's price every time she displayed it.

"I'm a rooster . . . I'll be a hen! Look at me: I'm a goose . . . I'm a rabbit . . . You be a lion . . . No, I'll be a stallion; watch out there, you pretty little mare!"

The orchestra began its music once more, with an increasingly frenzied rhythm that travestied the dignified court music in vogue, while men and women threw aside part of their clothing and writhed, postured, jumbled drunkenly together and were overcome with laughter.

Only the Duke of Malaga was aloof from the crowd, his eyes squinting in appraisal of Prospero's passage through the room with Francesca's shrinking form beside him. Swiftly, Alfredo cut a path through the indecent charade about him and moved on a diagonal to intercept his host. "I didn't expect you to begin her public instruction so soon," he remarked, licking his lips gently and surveying Francesca with hot eyes.

The Prince raised his eyebrow slightly and glanced at the girl. "She seems untouched by it," he returned.

"Yes! How modestly she lowers her eyes. She has the untouched, otherworldly manner of a nun," Alfredo said. "You should have dressed her so."

"Such common spice appeals to you," Prospero murmured, lazily. "Perhaps we can find something a little more exotic that will appeal to me." He nodded to one of the nearby musicians who crashed his cymbals deafeningly next to Alfredo's ears, and the Duke flung his hands up with a scream, Prospero smiled with amusement. "So there *is* something aside from bedding a woman that can draw a response from you," he remarked, and turned courteously to motion Francesca forward.

"Shall we rest for a moment and enjoy the spectacle?" he inquired solicitously, handing her to the chair next his own. As Francesca ducked her head in assent but looked only at the floor when she was seated, Prospero's lips twitched. "*You* do not enjoy it," he said seating himself beside her and still holding her hand in his. "Ah, that is a pity. It is really most diverting."

Francesca shook her head involuntarily and looked away, as his hand closed about hers compellingly. "Look at me!" Unwillingly, her eyes rose to his. He studied her briefly and released her hand suddenly. "Very well. I will not force you—yet," he decided, consideringly, "but since I have offered a prize, I must decide who will win it.

"Yes," she whispered. "That is only fair."

"And if nothing else, *I* am always fair and just," he remarked, with a chuckle. Francesca flushed and hung her head. Prospero patted her hand and laughed outright. "Oh, you are a delight, my dear! Very well then: I shall judge the contest and you may look—where you choose. I recommend the tapestries on the far wall. They are quite exceptional and well worth your attention."

"Close your eyes, my dear," he advised. "Now I shall decide on the winner—and then I shall take you away for a while—and sometime when we are alone and you are calmer, we will look at the tapestries together and I will explain the magnificent embroidery." He patted her hand again, casually, while his eyes roamed over the room and fastened on a man who'd announced himself a bull—and who was now most definitely and openly proving it

Elsie Lee

with a simpering little whore. Prince Prospero raised a finger, and a servant was instantly beside him.

"Yes, your Highness?"

"Ten ducats for the bull—when he is finished—and," Prospero drew a sapphire ring from his finger, "this for the . . . heifer."

"Certainly, *Excellenzia.*"

"So it is finished," the Prince said, rising and drawing Francesca with him. "Now we shall talk a while . . ." Briskly he led her away to carved doors that flew open at their approach, revealing a room furnished in shades of yellow.

"Oh, how lovely!" she said involuntarily, staring about her with awe. "It is like the sun."

"My father once imprisoned someone here for three years," the Prince observed, glancing about him casually. "When the man was released he could never again bear to look at the sun . . . nor even at a daffodil."

"How cruel!" Francesca said indignantly.

"It was simply a test to prove how easily a man's mind can be controlled and twisted," Prospero told her, instructively. "My family has always been interested in such things. Somewhere in the human mind is the key to our existence. My ancestors tried to find it, to open the door that seaparated us from our creator."

"You need no doors to find God, if you believe," Francesca began, but the Prince only shrugged with a cynical smile of mild amusement.

"If you believe, you are gullible," he said flatly. "Can you look around this world and believe in the goodness of a God who rules it? No! Famine, pestilence, war and death rule this world." He turned and went to open a farther door, while Francesca twisted her hands together and sought for words. Unconsciously, concentrating on the defense of what she felt to be indisputable, she followed Prince Prospero. "There is also love, and life, and hope," she said definitely, only half-seeing the room before her.

It was furnished entirely in shades of purple: Lilac, violet, lavender, and as the Prince ushered her into it, the golden fabric of Juliana's gown blended dramatically with the rich colorings. Prospero stood still for a moment, appreciating the contrast and

64

admiring the picture of Francesca's earnestness.

"There's very little hope, I assure you," he said absently. "Move a pace to the right, Please. Yes! That is exactly the best effect. No," he went back to the original conversation, "if a God of love and life did exist, he is long since dead. Someone or something else rules in his place."

He went past her again, to another door, and this room was pure white—but as Francesca's eyes went around it, they spied one discordant note: a door, dead-black and carved into strange symbols that split the purity of one white wall like the thumbprint of Satan. Instinctively curious, Francesca moved toward it. Behind her, Prospero's voice said, "No! That door is not open to you—yet."

She paused and looked over her shoulder, bewildered by the expression of mingled fear and adoration on his face. Drawing back, she said, "What is in there? You look as though . . ." She hesitated, searching for words. "Is there something to fear in that room?"

Prospero came forward and passed her to lay his hand lightly, caressingly, on the carvings of the door. "For the uninvited there is much to fear," he murmured, almost lovingly, and turned away. "But this has been a trying day for you," he said, briskly affectionate. "You must sleep. In the morning you may see Gino and your father."

Francesca looked up at the impassive dark eyes searchingly, but Prospero's face was suddenly tender as a father's. He put his arms about her gently, and unconsciously she responded with a brilliant smile. *"Thank you your Highness!"* she whispered, leaning her forehead against his shoulder briefly. "Oh, perhaps you are kind, after all.

"Indeed I am the very essence of—kindness," the deep voice promised softly, but in her weariness Francesca missed the cynical amusement in his tone. Leaning against the strong protective arm that led her to the door through the purple and yellow rooms and up the staircase to the bedchamber—Francesca was already half-asleep . . .

Chapter V

NOW THE CASTLE SLEPT, from Luigi snoring like a foghorn in the cubbyhole beside the chains for the drawbridge, to Bertrand and Guglielmo in the guard room among their companions—except Josef, who had slid away silently into the darkness of the courtyard and staircases on a mission of his own not unconnected with Donna Esterra.

In the castle stables, the horses stamped their feet and shuffled sleepily while the stable boys burrowed into their straw pallets and dreamed of beautiful girls, gigantic roasts of meat, unlimited wine and beautiful girls. In the kitchen quarters, Arturo's subconscious presented him with a new and revolutionary way to serve roast baby wood boar: with an apple in its mouth! He turned ecstatically on his side and whined in his slumbers.

Here and there, night torches illuminated staircases and corridors dimly, while Louis followed the prescribed route for the night watch—not that there would be anything to find, he yawned mightily, aside from a guest who'd drunk too much and crawled behind one of the tapestries to sleep it off. Methodically, he lifted each of the wall hangings and held his torch high, but for once there was no somnolent figure to be carted off to a chamber. Coming into the guard room at last, Louis handed his torch to the sleepy youngster who would take the next tour. "Two of the clock, and all's well," he said, and stretched himself with another gigantic yawn and shake. "I'm for bed; you can go out at three, Marco, but it's an easy night. Not a soul stirring."

"Good!" the other guard said fervently. "Sleep well, Louis."

With a raised hand, Louis stumbled off to his cot. There'd be four hours before he need get up again, and thank God, in spite of the wild party in the great hall, there'd been no incidents tonight . . .

But although the castle seemed to sleep, there were those who tossed and turned, who waked and stared into the darkness, or those who sobbed softly—such as Esmeralda, lying on her child-sized bed at the top of the castle. The room was tiny, yet magnificently large for the midget ballerina! In a corner lay the grayhound, quiescent and watching every motion of its mistress, while Hop-Toad knelt awkwardly beside the bed.

"Shhh," he muttered under his breath. "Now, now, don't cry! It was not your fault, it was only a nasty accident, shhhh." Tentatively, he stretched a hand to touch her head, and she jerked away wildly. "I'm sorry!" he said, instantly apologetic. "Forgive me. I know my touch . . ."

"Is gentle and kind," she whispered, turning to grasp his hand and look into his eyes. "You misunderstood: I cry for you as well as myself."

"Don't cry for me," he said, infinitely pained. "I'm worth nothing."

Esmeralda stared at him earnestly. "You—are worth everything." she murmured. "In all the world, there is only you who have ever touched me with . . ." She hesitated, seeking the right words, while Hop-Toad leaned forward, gently urging her to speak—scarcely daring to hope . . .

"Yes? Tell me," he breathed. "I have touched you . . ."

"With affection and love," she finished softly, and smiled brilliantly at the deformed jester. "How cruel they are to creatures small and weak as we," she sighed sadly, while Hop-Toad bent his head to kiss her hand, to hold it gently against his cheek. Finally, he stood up, drawing his crooked back as straight as possible.

"I feel as tall as any man in the world," he said quietly. "No one will ever strike you again, I swear it." His eyes held hers hypnotically. "Would you be afraid to go with me? he asked, almost conversationally. "Away from here, out into the world?"

"I would go anywhere in—or out—of this world with you," she

whispered, and held out her arms . . .

In Juliana's bedroom, Francesca slept beneath a great canopy and stirred fitful, turning and tossing, half-awaking with the unaccustomed night light that burned on the bedside table above the small cross the Prince had bade her remove earlier. As she disrobed and climbed into the huge bed, Francesca's hand reached involuntarily to lie gently over her talisman. For the moment, she was half-minded to hold it in her hand and take it to bed with her—but the Prince had said she was never to wear it in the castle, and he had promised she would see Gino and Ludovico tomorrow. Almost, he had seemed kindly disposed toward her.

Better to take no chances, she decided. Let the cross lie where he had placed it; God and the Saviour would understand what was in her heart. Momentarily comforted, Francesca slid beneath the cool sheets that were so fine-woven, so unlike anything she'd ever known before. Wonderingly, her fingers felt the soft smoothness of texture before she pulled the down quilt to her shoulders. Instinctively she snuggled into the bed; if *this* were luxury, there was no denying it was very pleasant. Francesca sighed deeply—and was instantly asleep.

She knew not when, nor why, she awoke. It seemed as though an unidentifiable shadow had moved across her face, briefly coming between her and the flickering candle of the night light—and then drifting away so that the candle light forced itself within her closed eyelids. Her ears seemed to hear the definitive click of a softly closed door.

But surely she had locked and bolted her door before going to bed?

Francesca was instantly wide awake, every nerve taut, her eyes peering fearfully out into the room. With an effort at courage, she sat bolt upright in the bed, gathering the coverlets up to her neck and quavering, "Who's there?"

There was no answer—yet she *felt* an alien presence.

Staring wildly into the shadowy corners of the room, her eyes conjured up demons, devils, in every piece of furniture. It seemed that a great dark, cloaked and hooded figure stood in one corner, glaring redly at her. With a gasp of terror, she reached for the candlestick and held it forward to illumine that corner—and found the menacing apparition was no more than a dressing gown hung on the clothes rack!

"Oh!" she sighed, almost giggling in the relief of tension . . . for of course it was all only a nightmare; the door was secured, and no one could possibly have been in the room. Turning, she began to replace the candlestick on the night table—and stopped abruptly. Raising the ornate silver holder again, she stared intently at he night table, feeling a shiver of horror working up her spine.

The cross was gone.

In its place was a small pool of liquid. Francesca forced herself to study it closely, and there was no doubt about it.

The liquid was blood.

With a gasp, Francesca withdrew her hand sharply, and in the swiftness of her motion, the flame flickered and died. *"Ave Maria, Sancta Maria, ora pro nobis . . ."* she babbled wildly, and banged the candlestick down upon the table, to throw back the bed coverings and scramble frantically from the far side of the bed. For a moment she crouched, her heart pounding with terror, staring cautiously about the room.

There was no doubt that she was alone. Neither was there any doubt that, despite her care in barring the door, *someone* had entered during her sleep and removed the precious protection of her cross. *"Jesù,* save me!" she prayed silently, and found strength to move, to stand erect beside the bed. As she stood, the final smoldering log in the fireplace broke apart into a shower of tiny sparkles and collapsed in ashes. With a deep sob of fright, Francesca flew across the room, grabbing the dressing robe as she passed and throwing wide the door in her dead panic.

In the corridor outside, she struggled into the gown and looked at the yawning door in horror—because it should have been barred and bolted, yet it had opened smoothly at her lightest touch.

Every connected thought and memory was erased from her mind in the terror of the moment. Francesca looked hastily from one side to the other and could recall nothing of the directions within the castle. Which way to go, where to find help? Without her cross, Francesca was only a terrified peasant girl again, shivering and whimpering like a hunted animal. At random—for there was only blackness whichever way she looked—she raced along the hallway, her hand sliding along the smooth panelling until it connected with startling suddenness against the carved top newel of the staircase down which she had followed Juliana.

Briefly she clung to it, listening—but there were no footsteps, no pursuit, only the sound of her own heartbeat. Automatically, her foot felt cautiously for the first step of the staircase, while she tried to calm herself. Then, swiftly she ran downward, letting her hand slide along the polished balustrade, ready to grip at any moment if she missed her footing. Rounding a curve, she glimpsed the great branched standing candelabra, fully lit at the bottom of the stairs. With a sob of relief, Francesca raced down the final steps and fell gasping against the towering newel post ending the handrail. At least, there was light—yet as she cowered beneath the flickering candles, pushing back her tumbled hair, she was still uncertain and disoriented.

Tremulously, she sagged against the stairs and tried to catch her breath. Ahead in the dimness, she thought she recognized the heavy damask curtains of the entrance to the main hall through which Prince Prospero had led her during the orgy of his guests. She remembered the immensity of the room with its high vaulted ceiling, and shivered; it had been horrible enough when the sconces blazed with hundreds of candles—double dreadful now, when it was still and darkened.

Yet which way to turn? In the silence, she was conscious of the steady ticking of the clock, somewhere to her left, shrouded in darkness—but where the clock had brought anxiety and uneasiness to Prospero's guests, it was comforting reassurance to Francesca.

For a long moment, she huddled in her dressing gown on the bottom step of the stairs, wrapping the folds of cloth about her bare feet against the chill of the marble hall floor. She breathed evenly in a rhythm to match the clock. Almost, she had fallen asleep against the bannisters when she realized there was another—sound. It was thin, moaning, a sort of counterpoint to the faithful tick of the clock. Francesca raised her head and listened alertly. It seemed to emanate from the right, while the clock was definitely to her left.

Hesitantly, she rose and stole toward the door beyond the hall candelabra, shivering as her bare feet encountered the cold marble, but as she cautiously peered beyond the door, she went forward more confidently. Within was the Yellow Room the Prince had shown her previously. It was fully lighted, ablaze with candles.

Someone was evidently awake. Francesca felt her feet sinking gratefully into the warmth of the beautiful carpet that covered the floor, and simultaneously it seemed that the strange keening moan that had accompanied the clock was now more like organ music rising and falling weirdly. She could no longer hear the clock; the hall door had fallen shut behind her, but she was not dismayed.

Now she remembered that beyond the Yellow Room was a Purple Room. Quietly, Francesca went swiftly over the royal purple carpet and opened the door to the White Room, to find it lit by only a single candle. Now the Black Door was slightly ajar and a blood red light laid a slender fan upon the white rug. She ran across to push the door tentatively, but it swung open soundlessly beneath her light touch, and instinctively, she stepped back, pressing a hand to her mouth.

The room within was completely black, but for a blood-red window set above an altar from which issued the vivid illumination. It seemed to be some sort of fire, that flickered and leapt unseen, although it created enough light to see quite clearly the strange cabalistic and Satanic symbols decorating the walls.

Directly facing Francesca was a carved ebony throne and upon it, garbed in dead black and staring straight at the intruder, sat Juliana!

Francesca recoiled a few steps farther, and suppressed a scream, but Juliana sat motionless. Although her eyes seemed to stare at Francesca, in fact they were tranced and unseeing. Realizing the woman was actually unaware of her, curiosity got the better of Francesca's common-sense. She crept forward and peered about the edge of the door. It swung even farther open, and she was facing a catafalque topped by a black coffin. At each corner burned a huge black candle on a single stand.

What a strange sort of funeral, Francesca thought confusedly, and went forward to peek into the open casket, only to gasp with incredulity—*for within lay Prince prospero.* Clad in black velvet, his face was deadly pallid against the black satin ruching that lined the casket.

Could it be *true* that the evil genius of Estaban was dead! Tremulously, Francesca fled . . . racing through the series of rooms and struggling with the doors that had opened so easily before but which now seemed perversely determined to prevent her retreat. Behind her there was the sound of distant shrill laughter, as she reached the main hall with the staircase and the standing candelabra. Sobbing in terror, she thought only of her bedchamber and the safety of a bolted door. Completely forgetting that an unbolted door was what had led her to leave it in the first place, she whirled frantically up the stairs, dragging herself along with a firm grasp on the handrail.

In the upper hall, she gasped for support, a second to catch her breath. Her hand met only heavy cloth draperies, pulling them aside—and within was a grinning horror, leering at her and laughing drunkenly. Her last reserves of strength broke, and Francesca screamed and screamed at the top of her healthy peasant lungs—until the horrible face was suddenly removed.

It was only a mask, covering the Duke of Malaga who reached toward her tipsily and said, "Did I startle you, my dear?"

Breathlessly, she thrust past him and raced to her room, heedless of his angry cries as he tumbled against the hard stone of the embrasure. Behind her she could hear him recovering, pursuing in unsteady but determined footsteps, but she'd found her door and darted within, to slam and bolt it in one deft motion. Briefly, she leaned against the door jamb, all her energy spent while Alfredo beat vigorously on the outside of the door and twisted the handle angrily.

Deliberately, Francesca turned the key in the lock and ignored the Duke's furious shouts. Backing away, she assessed the door as proof against anything less than a crowbar. In the outer corridor she could hear another masculine voice and momentarily her heart pounded anxiously, but it was evidently only a castle guard on his rounds. In voluntarily, her lips twitched in a faint smile as she heard Alfredo, Duke of Malaga, attempting to convince the guard that everything was completely under control, merely a mistake in his room—while the guard most firmly and politely insisted upon escorting the Duke to his own quarters.

As their voices died away along the corridor, she turned wearily toward the bed. On the night table, the candle flickered softly; in the fireplace, the last embers sparkled among the ashes. The bedclothes were neatly turned back, awaiting her . . .

Francesca stood still and stared, feeling terror creeping over her again—because the candle should have been unlit, the bedsheets should hare been dragged untidily from the bed . . . and upon the night table there should be a pool of blood where formerly her treasured cross had lain. She took two steps forward and peered at the table.

Beneath the candlelight, the polished wood of the cross gleamed delicately. There was no sign of blood. Francesca put her hands over her face and tried to think. Could it be only a dream? Was she in the midst of a nightmare mentally, while perhaps her body was still lying in the luxurious bed beneath the fine sheets and soft down quilt? Cautiously she parted her fingers and peered at the bed—and indeed it did seem there was a shadowy form lying there . . .

With a moan, Francesca fainted.

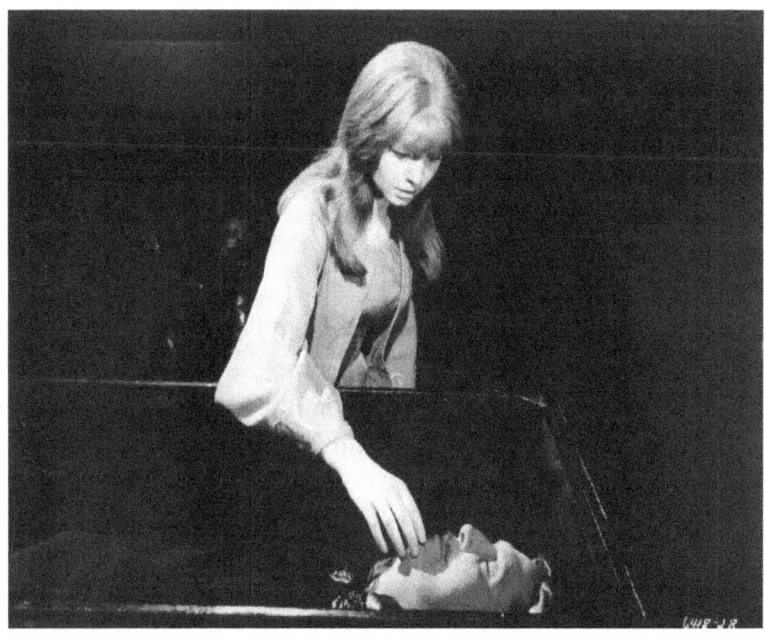

Chapter VI

FROM THE BATTLEMENTS of the castle, one could see the countryside stretching out in miles of rolling hills, interspersed with patches of tilled fields and small woods, bisected here and there by highways and country lanes. After one glance, Francesca resolutely turned her back to the faint curls of smoke hanging lazily over the ashes of Estaban. Beside her, Prince Prospero held a falcon on his gloved wrist, stroking its feathers while he eyed her closely with the gaze a pedagogue would turn upon a prized student.

"You look pale and drawn."

"I slept badly. I dreamed—or thought I dreamed," she said nervously, still wondering whether the events of the previous night were not simply a dream. Yet, she *had* wakened on the floor, as if from a faint . . .

"Yes? You dreamed . . . ?" Prospero urged gently.

"A room. A black room with candles burning," she shivered in memory. "It was filled with destruction and death and evil."

"Often the appearance of 'evil' is simply a lack of understanding," Prospero commented. Looking out into the sky, he suddenly took the hood from the falcon and slipped the hesses. Instantly the bird rose from his wrist.

"Watch!"

Francesca stood silent, mesmerized by the beauty in the falcon's swift soaring curve. It overtopped a passing pigeon, then swooped to the kill and struck in a small explosion of feathers. Returning, the falcon dropped the dead bird at Prospero's feet and resumed its seat on his wrist.

"Do you know how a falcon is trained?" the Prince asked. Francesca shook her head, mutely, averting her eyes from the dead pigeon. "His eyes are sewn shut. Blinded temporarily, he suffers the whims of his God, patiently, until his will is submerged and he learns to serve. Thus your God taught and blinded you with crosses."

"You had me take off my cross because it offended . . ."

"Offended no one," Prospero interrupted gently. "My Master and his followers look about with open eyes. It just appeared to me—discourteous—to wear the symbol of a deity long dead."

"Your master?" she repeated fearfully.

"Satan," he said, casually. "The Lord of Flies, the Fallen Angel, the Devil."

While Francesca still stared at him, there was the sound of coach wheels approaching along the road below. The outrider's horn blasted three long hoots. Prospero drew her with him to look over the parapet just as the coach drew to a stop.

"Who seeks entrance to Prince Prospero's castle?" he called down, and a man stuck his head from the coach window.

"Scarlatti and his wife, Prospero's invited guests! Open the gate and lower the bridge at once."

"This is the prince himself that speaks to you, Scarlatti. You're overdue."

Scarlatti shielded his eyes and peered upward unsteadily. He was evidently slightly drunk. "Some business that could not wait," he apologized, "but we hurried on as soon as we could by the most direct route."

"The most direct? You passed through the village?"

"Yes. It was burned to the ground."

"Be on your way!" Prospero said firmly.

"I don't understand," Scarlatti began, confusedly.

"You are no longer welcome here!"

Huffily, Scarlotti clambered out of the coach and stared up. "Now, really! I know your whims, but you invited . . ."

"The village is full of the Red Death," Prospero cut in sharply.

"The Red Death!" Scarlatti repeated, white-faced and instantly sobered, while his wife's stricken face appeared at the open coach door. "I beg you, Prince Prospero," Scarlatti shouted, "allow us haven! I beg sanctuary."

"This is no Christian church."

"In the name of any God of all the Gods of time," Scarlatti insisted, "I beg you!" With a sudden thought he clutched his wife's arm and dragged her from the coach so hastily that she tripped and sprawled upon the ground, her wrist still in his grasp. "My wife— you always thought her beautiful," Scarlatti babbled desperately. "Oh, I new you desired her. I watched you follow her with your eyes. She is beautiful, you must admit that—and she knows how to please a man . . ."

Prospero ignored him with a shrug. "This Scarlatti thought himself one of your 'good' men. He thought his wife pure and unassailable," he remarked to Francesca, just as Scarlatti's voice came loud and clear.

"I give her to you to do with as you please!"

Prospero looked over the parapet with an implacable expression, and called down, "I have already had the doubtful pleasure."

Signora Scarlatti pulled herself to her feet and shook herself free of her husband's clasp, eyeing him with contempt as he implored abjectly, "Prince, spare me the Red Death. I beg you—in the name of friendship . . ."

Prospero set the falcon on a nearby spike and calmly reached for a crossbow hung in readiness on the wall.

"In the name of friendship . . ." Scarlatti's voice wailed, and the Prince swiftly raised the crossbow and fired the bolt. It struck the man squarely in the throat, and he fell at his wife's feet.

"For you, friend!" Prospero said softly, and took the knife from his belt sheath, as Francesca stood transfixed with horror. Leaning over the parapet, he tossed the knife downward. "Spare yourself the Red Death, signora . . ."

Replacing the crossbow on its spike and taking the falcon back onto his wrist, the Prince observed Francesca's expression with faint amusement. "No doubt you think me the reverse of friendly at this moment," he remarked indolently, "but consider whether instant death might not be an act of the most Christian mercy in comparison to the Red Death."

Francesca stood her ground. "I think that is a decision not yours to make," she said, troubled.

"Whose, then?" he asked in surprise.

She shook her head. "I cannot compete with you in words, your Highness," she said sadly. "I have not the learning . . ."

"No more you have," he agreed pleasantly, "so let us agree to disagree for the moment, and speak of other things. You may choose the topic."Francesca bit her lips tremulously. "You—did promise . . . that I should see Gino and my father this morning." she reminded him in a breathless rush of words.

"Why, so I did." Prospero's tone was soft, and he eyed the girl's pleading expression with a sudden laugh. "And so you shall! Come . . ."

Oddly enough, Prince Prospero's original words to Francesca, that Gino and Ludovico were berthed in a safe warm place, were more or less true, for it was no part of his plan to starve or harm the two men until they should have served his purpose for entertainment. True, they were thrust into a dungeon below ground, but there had been a plate of warm meat scraps for an evening meal, and beyond the barred door, the guard room fire had provided just sufficient heat to lessen the graveyard chill of the cold stone cell.

Aside from their loss of freedom and the anxiety for Francesca, Gino thought philosophically that they were not badly off. The straw pallets in the cell were no worse than what they were accustomed to use, and their peasant cottages often no warmer than this, while fresh-cooked meat was a definite rarity in their lives. If it were not for his mental turmoil, Gino might even have enjoyed his situation, but from long acquaintance with His Highness, there was no doubt in Gino's mind that ahead lay unimaginable trial and tribulation.

In a sort of wordless communication, Gino and Ludovico sat silently in their cell, saying nothing of the apprehension in their minds. When they had finished the meat scraps and thrust the trenchers through the bars, Ludovico said only, "We should sleep, to gather strength," and forthwith curled himself upon his pallet, closing his eyes firmly. That made sense to Gino, also.

They roused to the morning interchange between the men in

the guard room, and silently accepted the trenchers of hot mush and cold meat scraps, eating stolidly—still wordlessly agreed on gathering what strength they could for whatever might lie ahead. It was mid-morning, although they had lost all sense of time since they could see the sun, when a guard opened the cell door and said, "Come on."

Flanked by two stalwart guards, Gino and Ludovico were led away to another stone-floored room. It was the armory, hung with swords and shields on every wall. Briefly, the men stood and stared about them, while the fetters were unlocked from wrists and ankles. Facing them were two more guards, clad in leather practice jerkins and armed with swords. The guards who had led them from the cell now briskly thrust one of the wall swords into each hand, and moved off, to stand with folded arms against the entrance door. "Here they are: all yours, Josef!" they called, and composed themselves comfortably to view the spectacle.

The handsomer of the two armed guards swaggered forward a few paces and inspected Gino carefully. "I'll take this one, he looks to have spirit," he said over his shoulder. "You take the other one, Louis." Pursing his lips, Josef felt Gino's muscular arm with a practiced hand. "Yes, you'll do," he decided, and moved back a few paces. "Now, watch me! Set your feet like mine, and grasp the sword in your hand like this . . ."

Gino stood motionless, a dim memory from his few years of schooling at the monastery rising in his mind. What had the good brothers called them, those pagans who were forced to fight each other in ancient Rome before Our Saviour had come to bring light to the world? He could not remember the name—but it was positive to his horrified mind that *this* was the spectacle planned by Prince Prospero: that Gino should fight his intended father-in-law.

Instinctively, he discarded the sword, ringingly on the stone floor, and Ludovico immediately followed. Josef looked at them impatiently. "Pick it up! We're ordered to train you in the use of arms."

"So my friend and I can hack each other to death for the pleasure of Prospero's guests?" Gino inquired evenly.

"Don't be a fool," Louis interposed. "One of you could survive, and if you fight well, the living one might be given his freedom."

"Like you? One of Prospero's pet dogs?" Gino countered, and stood his ground as Louis moved forward in fury at the insult. "Kill me," said Gino coolly, "and I'm sure Prospero will see you dead for ruining his entertainment."

Louis paused briefly. "I won't kill you," he snarled, "just cut you a bit . . ." and lashed out with his long blade, marking a neat line across Gino's forehead, while Josef said judicially, "A very expert wound, Louis. Bravo!" As the blood slowly welled from the scratch, Gino simply stood—stoically. Now thoroughly angry, Louis grinned like a wolf and made a skillful pass with his sword, ripping through Gino's ragged shirt and slashing a shallow wound across his chest. Gino's eyes smouldered dangerously, but still he stood motionless, while Louis delicately completed a crosscut on his bare chest and the other guards murmured approval.

Now Gino's own temper suddenly exploded. Diving forward, he grasped the sword he'd discarded previously, and as Louis moved toward him, rolled lithely aside and up to his feet, to strike furiously at the guard.

Louis only smiled and made a casual swipe that left a fine red line across Gino's shoulder, but Gino was beyond control. He leaped to the wall and grabbed a leather shield, while Louis almost laughingly put forth a series of massive blows that drove Gino backward, to stumble and fall. The guard stood over him and thrust repeatedly; Gino managed to catch all the blows on his shield, as the other guards shouted encouragement and Ludovico stood quietly aside from the fray.

Suddenly, the door opened and the two guards on either side sprang to attention as Prospero entered, leading Francesca. Gino was cowering under his shield, avoiding Louis's furious swipes and passes. "No!" she protested wildly, grabbing the Prince's arm tightly. "Stop them! *Please* stop them; Gino knows nothing of fighting . . ."

Prospero held her protectively in the doorway and viewed the scene with amusement—and suddenly Gino had thrust out a skillful foot to trip Louis, scrambling to his feet while the guard rolled away out of reach. "But he learns rather fast," the Prince commented casually, his eyes flicking from one to the other of the antagonists with growing interest.

There was no doubt Gino did learn fast! With no training, no knowledge of ethical swordplay, armed only with sheer fury, he was attacking Louis full force and no holds barred. The other guards stood tense and glanced at Prince Prospero for a sign to spring to Louis's aid—and instead, His Highness's slender fingers imperiously restrained them, while Francesca clung to his arm and felt a surge of confidence, as Gino forced the guard back and back.

Louis had grabbed a shield and was no longer smiling, but defending himself vigorously, as Gino literally swarmed all over him. Ludovico moved gently along the wall, out of the way, and Josef stood easily, observing the fracas with the same impartial interest as Prospero. Nor did his impassivity alter when Gino, with a blow of driving ferocity, knocked Louis's sword from his hand, leaving the guard pinned against the farther wall behind his shield. With two swift paces, Gino tore away the shield and set the point of his sword at Louis's throat.

In the minute silence, Prince Prospero said coolly, "You see, it's a true fact that the greatest swordsman in Italy would not fear the second greatest, but would fear the worst—for that one would be unpredictable."

Gino lowered his blade from Louis ashen face, and turned to drop his sword and shield contemptuously, sliding them across the stone floor to clatter at Prospero's feet. His eyes flickered at the sight of Francesca, standing beside the Prince, and he took a few impulsive steps toward her. Instantly, the door guards moved to intercept him, and Gino stopped.

"Francesca!" he said quietly. "Are you all right?"

"*Yes,* Gino!" she told him firmly, with a wealth of meaning in her voice. "And you?"

His hand indicated the blood on forehead and chest. "A few scratches given me to taunt me to fight," he shrugged, and stared defiantly at Prospero, "but I will not fight my friend."

"You may force me to discipline you in some other way," the Prince murmured thoughtfully.

"Do what you will," Gino retorted.

"Nor will I fight," Ludovico spoke almost in the same breath.

"And I don't think you'll give us up for simple torture," Gino remarked with native shrewdness, "because then you would have been in some way defeated."

Prince Prospero studied the young peasant with a grudging respect for his insight. "You surprise me," he admitted, "but I'm pleased to find you've given me a puzzle to think about. Yes," he reflected, half-smiling, "a very pretty problem. I shall enjoy solving it, although in the end, you two will challenge death together. You may be certain of that! Meanwhile," he glanced at the guards compellingly, "you will make certain these—guests will be cared for tenderly. No reprisals, you understand? Not even a harsh word. The best food, a small cup of wine, a warm jerkin for each." Thoughtfully, his Highness surveyed the two stolid figures of Gino and Ludovico, standing side by side with dignity and chins firmly *up*. "Yes," he drawled, "a pleasant puzzle—and let nothing interfere with my solution of it!"

Turning away, he drew Francesca's trembling figure with him. She had time only for one last loving smile of encouragement for the two men in her life before she found herself in the outer corridor, walking along silently beside the Prince. She was conscious of conflicting emotions: on the one hand, burning pride in Gino's success against the guard—and on the other, a terrible weak fear of this suave man beside her.

I will lift mine eyes unto the hills from whence cometh my strength, she thought vaguely—but she was already on a hill and the only strength belonged to Prospero. Lost in thought, she hurried along, keeping pace with his long legs until she faced a transverse corridor. Instinctively, she turned right and felt his hand on her arm.

"No, this way, my dear. It would be better," the soft voice murmured, and as she paused in confusion, there was a low moan from the passageway ahead of her. With a gulp, Francesca whirled and half-ran down the corridor he indicated—but suddenly she realized it was lined with a row of empty torture chambers. Trembling, she averted her head and felt his hand on her shoulder.

"I understand. Life is often ugly."

"But to torture *men*," she said, fiercely, completely forgetting herself. "Is this what your Master Satan demands as worship?"

His hand pulled her to stop briefly. "These cells are very old. A hundred years ago, and ancestor of mine was a Christian monk," Prospero stated, impersonally. "He was made examiner of an early Inquisition. In those cells, he tortured more than six hundred men, women, even children, to save their souls—for your God of Love."

Francesca looked up at him despairingly. "I can't answer you; you know we agreed I hadn't the knowledge," she said simply. "But is Satan a God of Hate, then?"

"Of reality, of truth!" he corrected her. "The world lives in despair and pain but is at least kept alive by a few men. If they lost their power, chaos would engulf everything. Sometimes that power must be used to teach harsh lessons."

"I don't want to learn," she whispered involuntarily. "I'm afraid"

"I have no wish to hurt you, my dear," Prospero said paternally. "Don't you understand? I'm a missionary, if you like. I want to help you save your soul, so you may join me in the real glory of Hell."

"No, never! she cried, shrinking away.

"The way is not easy, I know," he said indulgently, "but only give me your hand, and I shall lead you through the cruel light into the velvet darkness."

Turning, he faced her and extended his hand gracefully, while Francesca leaned back against the cold stone of the corridor walls and looked at him fearfully. The dark eyes were kindly once more, the hand was waiting—almost Francesca was hypnotized into setting her own within his clasp. Tentatively, her hand had begun to flutter toward his, when the great clock in the hall overhead struck sonorously. With a start, Francesca snatched away her hand and cried, "No! I can live only in the sunlight of God's goodness and kindness. I want no darkness, no!

With a sob, she slid along the wall away from his outstretched hand and fled wildly to the end of the corridor, up the narrow stone staircase, to find herself in the marble-floored main hall that was filled with the majestic ticking of the clock. Now she knew where she was, could spare a pat for the polished wooden case as she ran past it, and upward to the safety of her locked bedchamber . . .

Chapter VII

IN THE BEDROOM CORRIDOR, Hop-Toad sat on the ban-nister of the main staircase, swinging his legs and waiting. Suddenly one of the doors opposite flung open and Alfredo strode out. He paused with an immediate frown for the dwarf, who regarded him with an evil, taunting grin.

"What are you lurking about for, you twisted little devil?" the Duke demanded.

"Not only am I afflicted with this body but with sleeplessness during the siesta as well," Hop-Toad shrugged.

"Are you losing your sleep because of that midget dancer?" Alfredo smiled contemptuously.

Hop-Toad leaped nimbly from the bannister and drew himself erect as possible. "She's nothing to me," he said disdainfully, "I like a full-sized woman."

"Do you now?" Alfredo guffawed heartily. "And where would you go about getting such a woman?"

"My master, Prospero, provides me with companions from time to time," Hop-Toad simpered slyly.

"A good master!"

Hop-Toad shuffled his feet slightly, "Yes, I suppose so," he observed, but his tone left no doubt of uncertainty on the point. "I imagine there are better."

"Oh? You'd like to leave Prospero's service?"

Hop-Toad looked about him cautiously and leaned toward the Duke. "I fear for the security of his reign," he muttered. "If I could find a strong protector, I might dare a change."

"And what special services can you offer that would convince someone else to take you under his protection?" Alfredo asked, cynically.

"All manner of things," Hop-Toad assured him eagerly. "I've a crafty and inventive mind!"

"For example . . ."

"This masquerade," the dwarf said promptly. "*I* would devise something startling, novel—something that would be the talk of the entire revel."

"Have you told this novel thing to Prospero?"

"I fear the Prince is much to austere," Hop-Toad shook his head sadly.

"Hmmmm," the Duke raised his eyebrows and leaned back comfortably against his bedroom door. "Will you tell me?" As Hop-Toad looked dubious, Alfredo's hand stole into a pocket and jingling coins rang across the silence.

"Well," said the dwarf, capitulating at once, "everyone will dress as usual: Harlequin, or a Chinese mandarin, soldiers, princesses and so on. They will all be either beautiful or humorous—but all will obviously be human."

"I'll come as a demon," Alfredo countered, yawning lazily,

"Why not come as a great ape?" Hop-Toad asked softly, and acted it out. "When the guests are gathered, you would enter—arms swinging, moving toward the screaming ladies with lowered head and grinning jaw. It will be more than a costume; it will be a performance!"

"Hmmmm." The Duke fingered his chin thoughtfully, obviously caught by the idea. "Where would I get such a disguise?"

"There is one in the room of stuffed animals," Hop-Toad told him in an undertone. "Another toy Prince Prospero never bothers with any more—I'm sure it's forgotten." Bright-eyed, head cocked to one side, he watched Alfredo's narrowed eyes.

"You really think the idea would create a sensation?" the Duke inquired finally, turning to stroll away along the corridor. Swiftly Hop-Toad shambled alongside.

"Oh yes! And there's more to the game," he whispered, alluring. "Yes, much more! It will be the talk of the world, you'll see!"

Explaining eagerly in an undertone the dwarf trotted beside Alfredo until the pair were lost in the shadows . . .

While Prospero's guests happily rifled the armoires in the wardrobe rooms of the castle for gorgeous costumes in which to appear at the midnight masque, Francesca lay in exhausted sleep on her bed—and a single visitor stole into the Black Devil's Chapel, closing the door softly and going forward to kneel before the altar with its mysterious inner flames.

"Lord Satan," Juliana's voice was soft but intense, "he who is called Belial by the ancients—demon lover of those who wish to live in your eternal night, I call upon you! In this your hour of deepest dark, in your temple, before your altar I twice bind myself as you handmaiden and betrothed." Swiftly, her hand grasped the poignard lying beside the candlestick and drew its point deliberately in a vertical line down her bosom. As the blood drops sprang up, she looked up to the glowing red window above the altar and extended a cross, reversed. "With this symbol of your final and lasting victory I inscribe the final mark," she said huskily, and scratched a cross-piece in the lower quadrant of the bleeding line, to form an upside-down cross that was marked with blood drops.

"I offer myself to you," she whispered. "Send me a demon so I may know I'm to be your wife." Eyes closed, Juliana raised her face and waited—and as the great clock tolled the hour in the hall far behind her, it seemed there was a strange gust of air that blew out the candle, leaving only the altar flames. She opened her eyes and stared half-fearfully into the darkness, and there seemed a dancing shadow cast against the wall behind the altar and beneath the red window.

To Juliana's entranced eyes, it was a capering goat-like figure that raised its hand and beckoned . . .

With a moan of ecstasy, Juliana fell forward against the altar steps. For a long moment, she lay still, thinking furiously. Then she pulled herself to her feet and with downbent head, slipped backward to the door. "Thank you, Master!" she breathed, and slid into the White Room closing the black door firmly behind her. Turning, she hastened through the Purple and Yellow Rooms into the main hall, and up the staircase to her former bedroom.

After her wild retreat from Prince Prospero in the lower corridor of torture chambers, Francesca had paced back an forth in her room, twisting her hands together and praying fervently for the safety of Gino and her father. As the wintry sun set early in long slanting rays of pallid light striking coldly through the slit-windows of the chamber, a servant had brought a delicate plate of thin-sliced cold meats, a bowl of fruit, a wooden board furnished with a wedge of cheese and a crusty loaf of bread. From the cupboard beside the window, he produced a bottle of wine and a beautiful crystal goblet.

When all was set forth, the servants bowed themselves away. "Thank you," she said dully, and as the door closed, found herself sobbing wildly from the tension. Sinking to her knees beside the bed, she repeated the Ave Maria, closing her eyes and pretending the cross and rosary beads were slipping through her fingers.

For now the cross was most definitely missing from the night table where Prince Prospero had laid it the previous day, and from which, in her dream (if it were a dream?) it had been replaced by a pool of blood last night, although when Francesca had waked from her faint and crawled timidly back to bed, she had stroked it with a trembling finger beneath the candlestick. It had still been lying on the table this morning; now it was gone, and this could be no dream nor fevered fancy, for it was full daylight.

Francesca could accept the disappearance of her cross. Within her was an amazing confidence that sustained her in the anguish of mind for Gino and Ludovico. So her cross and been removed, she could still remember it, pretend to feel it, and Mary, Mother of Sorrows, would understand.

Over and over again, Francesca whispered, *"Ave Maria, gratia plena, dominus tectum, benedicta tu in mulieribus, et benedictus fructus ventris tui. Sancta Maria, Mater Dei, ora pro nobis peccatoribus nunc et in hora mortis nostrae."*

At last, exhaustedly, she rose from her knees and crawled shivering onto the bed, drawing up the down quilt and falling instantly asleep, while the modest fire died away to embers for lack of an extra faggot and the candlestick beside the dressing mirror flickered in a sly draft and went out.

She had no idea how long she had slept when her animal instincts alerted her to danger, and she was wide awake—lying motionless in the semi-darkness and aware that someone had opened her door, entered and closed the door softly . . . was even now softly approaching the bed. Paralyzed with fear, Francesca lay still, narrowing her eyes to mere slits through which she saw a hand gently parting the bed curtains.

It was a delicate white hand, and Francesca opened her eyes fully with a gasp of relief. "Juliana!" she sighed, propping herself on her elbow and trying to steady her pounding heart, "Thank God! I thought . . . I was afraid . . ."

"Yes?"

"I—don't know," Francesca murmured confusedly. "I simply couldn't move, and after all, it is only you . . . and you are my friend, really, are you not? You understand the terror all about me. I scarce know where I am nor what new horror may face me at any moment." Pushing back her tumbled hair with a weary hand, Francesca sat up cross-legged on the bed and looked trustfully at the older girl—with suddenly widened eyes. "What does that wound mean?" she whispered.

Juliana pulled the filmy scarf about her shoulders. "Satan's mark."

"Prospero did—*that* to you? Francesca's eyes flew to Juliana's in indignant compassion.

"I did it to myself," Juliana told her calmly. "It marks me as one of Satan's handmaidens." She shuddered violently and closed her eyes.

Francesca slid away from the bed and shrank back from the other girl. "You've given away your soul," she said finally in an undertone.

"Yes, gladly!"" Juliana said passionately. "Soon the last of my innocence will be gone and I shall have immortality—and I shall have Prospero as well." Momentarily, her eyes closed ecstatically as Francesca gazed at her in horror. Then she murmured, But I must be *certain.* " Her eyes flew open and fixed Francesca hypnotically. "If *you* were gone . . ."

"Would you dare to leave the safety of the castle?"

"There is no safety for me here," Francesca said, flatly.

Slowly Juliana extended her hand; on its palm lay a key." This will open the door to the cell. The guard on the north wall has been bribed and will let you down the other side. Take your Gino and your father, and *go!*"

"But the guards, the way through to the dungeons," Francesca whispered hesitantly.

"You've been to the armory, and the dungeons lie the other way," Juliana said impatiently. "Take the key, girl! For the rest, you must make your own way—or are you *afraid?*"

Swiftly, Francesca's hand swept the key from Juliana's and clutched it fiercely. "No, I am not afraid. I have a protector more powerful than yours," she hissed vehemently.

Juliana's eyes blazed at her angrily, then calmed into an expression of pitying superiority. "Rely upon Him, then, and be on your way as soon as possible, before the masque begins," she advised lightly, and swept away through the door before Francesca could say another word.

Left alone in the bedchamber, Francesca looked tremulously at the key in her hand: freedom—not only for herself but for her men. If only she had the courage, if only she could recall the twists and turns in the lower corridors. It did not enter her head to doubt Juliana's sincerity. As between one woman and another, even though Francesca might be a peasant she knew instinctively that Juliana's only goal was to be rid of the younger girl. Very probably, if Francesca failed to reach Gino and Ludovico, Juliana would pay a dreadful penalty for having tried to aid....

I must think, Francesca told herself firmly. *I must think first and plan carefully.* She forced herself to throw another log on the fire and sit down before it, to consider the task ahead. Closing her eyes in concentration, she went mentally down the main staircase to the hall with the great clock—but which was the door that led down to the corridor of the torture chambers?

Straight ahead would be the entrance to the banquet hall; to the right was the door to the Yellow Room. So far so good—but was the door leading to the dungeons next to that for the Yellow Room or beyond the clock? Francesca wracked her memory for that headlong flight from Prince Prospero that had brought her rushing through the hall and up to this room . . .

She had opened a door at the top of the dungeon staircase, but had she passed the clock or merely faced it as she whirled on up the stairs? *Think,* she told herself fiercely, *think!* Dimly she remembered: the door next to the Yellow Room led to the kitchen quarters—she recalled a servant going through it with a service of fresh wine as Prospero had led her away from the black door . . . and now she was positive she had run *past* the clock this afternoon.

So at the foot of the stairs, she would turn left and find the proper door just beyond the clock. Again, so far so good—but at the bottom of that staircase, which way to turn? *Go forward to the intersection,* said her mind, *and turn right for the armory.*

How she considered that room carefully: at the end of a short corridor, but only the one door through which she and Prospero had entered during the contest between Louis and Gino. So the men had been brought from somewhere to the left, from the extension of the corridor. That would be the turning from which Prospero had deterred her, from which had come the painful moan . . . Francesca shivered. She had no idea what lay in that direction. It would have to be chanced. With decision, she rose and found a dark cloak to cover herself completely.

At the door to the chamber, she stopped and crossed herself. "God—help me in the name of Your Son!" she whispered. Then, steadily and softly, she opened the door and stole into the hall.

It was lighted with flaring wall torches, but deserted at the moment. In the distance, Francesca could hear jovial voices, occasional burst of laughter: the guests preparing for the feast prior to the midnight masque. Swiftly, she went down the stairs, slipped past the clock to the doorway in the shadows behind it . . . and yes! She had been right! Before her was the long flight of stone steps, leading downward into dimness. In mingled terror and relief, Francesca felt her way onward with care, for here there were no torches.

Step by step, she descended and gradually found a faint lessening in the darkness ahead; a torch somewhere farther on must be casting a little light against the end of the corridor walls. Reconnoitering, she found again her memory had served her well, for there to the right was the door to the armory. What lay to the left?

Her heart pounding painfully at the sight. Across the stone corridor lay a wide path of brilliant light, coming from the guard room! Within she could hear male voices and movements. Francesca slid along the wall and peered very cautiously around the edge of the doorway.

There were two guards . . . the ones who had brought them to the castle . . . sitting at a table, eating bread and cheese. A carafe of wine stood beside them, with plain but generous-sized metal cups. They were evidently off-duty for the moment, and idly playing a dicing game. Just as Francesca was about to whisk across the light path, another guard emerged from an inner room and came toward the table. He was the guard Gino had bested in the armory, and instinctively one of the seated men started to turn and look up at him!

Francesca shot back and pinned herself against the wall, holding her breath, but apparently he hadn't seen her, for the conversation continued between the guards. She could hear the rattle of the dice cup, the thrown dice bouncing on the wooden table, while a voice said, "Pass over the wine, Guglielmo," and another asked, "What's o'clock, Louis?"

"Eight," the first voice returned, and there were splashing sounds as he filled his wine cup. "Who's winning—as if I needed to ask?"

"Bertrand, of course!"

Once more Francesca peered into the room, to find luck was with her, for the newcomer stood beside the guard whose back was to the door—and the two bodies effectually prevented a clear view to the guard facing the door. Swiftly, she moved across the farther wall, but there was no movement from the guards; the dicing and idle chatter went on. She'd made it safely!

All that remained now was to search for Gino and her father. Exhaling a silent breath of relief, Francesca went steadily forward, feeling her way carefully as the passageway grew darker. In the growing dimness, she saw a small cavernous stairway leading down. For a moment she hesitated; then she moved onward and eventually came out on a lower level lit by a couple of feeble torches. All around her were the chattering, skittering sounds of rats, and she shivered involuntarily.

Facing her was a long row of cells with a small grating in each. She paused at the first one and called softly, "Gino . . . father?" From within there was a dreadful whining moan and a clatter of chains. With a gulp of horror, she moved on to the next cell, whispering shakily, "Gino, where are you?" As she bent to the grating, trying to see into the darkness of the cell, a manacled hand and a wild staring face crashed against the iron bars directly before her. She leaped back and flung her hands over her mouth to stifle her squeal of terror. The poor creature gibbering at her was obviously mad.

Hurrying on, Francesca felt half-mad herself. Where could Gino be? "Gino, Gino?" she hissed wildly, and trembled with relief when his voice said, "Yes? Francesca?" His face appeared at a grating farther on, and she ran forward to insert Juliana's key with trembling fingers. The door swung open and his arms were about her at once. "How?" he whispered.

"Juliana!" Briefly she drew away to hug her father closely. "We must hurry to the battlements. The guard there has been bribed to help us, but no other guard has."

"We'll find our way past them," Gino reassured her, and in close formation, the three of them hastened back past the terrible cells, scattering the rats in mad flight before their feet. Up the staircase they went, pausing at the top.

There was still the lighted doorway to the guard room to be traversed. In the silence, they could hear the clink of the wine mugs, the rattle of the dice, the murmur of voices.

"How many?" Gino whispered in her ear.

"Three," Francesca mouthed at him, holding up three fingers.

"You must slip across first," Gino decided. "Come on."

Quietly, they moved along the wall and flattened themselves against it. Francesca looked at Gino, who nodded with an encouraging smile. She sped across the light, but this time she was not lucky. Within the guard room there was the scrape of a chair violently pushed back from the table.

"I *knew* I saw something besides a rat pass before!" said one voice, and hasty footsteps raced toward the door.

"You there—stop!" The guard called Guglielmo appeared, sword in hand, turning to follow Francesca's fleeing figure, with long strides. Ludovico leaped forward to grab the guard around the neck, grasping the sword arm in a steely grip at the same time.

Now Gino's morning adversary, Louis, appeared, also sword in hand, and Gino was instantly upon him . . .had whirled him around just as Bertrand reached the corridor. Using Louis as a shield, Gino pushed him forward as Bertrand thrust with his sword—and in the split-second timing, the guard captain was unable to check his lunge.

Louis groaned fearfully as Bertrand's sword stabbed through his stomach. As he sagged, dying, in Gino's grasp, Gino's hand ran up his wrist and wrenched away the sword. With one powerful heave, Gino tossed Louis's body across Bertrand's path, and as the guard captain stumbled, Gino dealt him a fierce two-handed blow with the sword directly across the neck. Bertrand fell silently, his head wobbling grotesquely on its broken neck, while Gino turned swiftly toward Ludovico.

Francesca's father needed no help. Even as Gino reached his side, Guglielmo slumped soundlessly onto the stone flags of the corridor, his face cyanotic from strangulation in Ludovico's pow-erful hands. "Quickly," Gino whispered, and together they sped after Francesca, who was standing tremulously at the base of the upper staircase.

This is the way to the walls," she said, pointing to an intersec-tion at the landing halfway up to the main hall. "I remember, we came down this way from the battlements this morning, before . . ." She shuddered, recalling Gino's fight in the armory.

"Shhh, don't think of it," he told her softly. "Up you go, and we follow you!

They crept up the stairs to yet another landing, where Gino's hand stayed Francesca briefly. Clutching the sword tightly, he slid around her and reconnoitered—sprang across the landing into the deep shadows of the far corner. Again, he paused and peered upward. Now there were only a dozen steps leading on, and above there was a star-filled square of sky beyond an open door. Gino looked back to the others and motioned them to follow him; once more they hurried up the stone steps.

Nearly at the top, Gino paused again, frowning in concentration. Now they could see the sky, feel the fresh cool outer air, observe the light mist wreathing about the parapet—but Gino was suddenly hesitant.

"What is it?" Francesca whispered, anxiously.

"Only three guards in all those corridors?" he muttered. "I like it not! Can this woman Juliana be trusted?"

There was a stricken silence. "Can any of these mad people?" Ludovico observed finally. "We have no choice."

"I suppose not," Gino agreed, and led the way forward crouching into the mist at the exit door.

Ahead of them stood the guard, poised on the battlements and looking out toward the castle approaches. Cautiously, the trio stole forward.

"Guard?" Gino asked softly, and the tall figure began to turn leisurely, its face hidden in the hooded cloak—until at last it faced them.

One hand threw back the hood revealing—*Prince Prospero.* As Francesca screamed involuntarily, there were pounding footsteps behind them. Gino and Ludovico whirled and prepared to fight, but Gino had been right in his mistrust at the lack of guards, for now there were a full dozen armed men. They fell upon Gino and Ludovico and beat them to the rooftop. Francesca ran forward to kneel beside them, sobbing. "Julina betrayed us . . ."

Prospero's hand dragged her ruthlessly to her feet. "No. She betrayed me!"

"What can you want of two men who've done you no harm?" Francesca demanded in anguish, clinging to his arm and shaking ti furiously.

"They killed three of my guards," the Prince replied blandly, holding her still. "Three human beings. According to your faith, they have sinned greatly—and tonight at the feast before the masque, at least one will pay for those sins."

Chapter VIII

THE GREAT BANQUET HALL blazed with lighted candles, but the guests were more glittering than the tapers. Assembled for the feast before donning masquerade costumes, their gowns and suits were gorgeous beyond anything Francesca had ever seen. The wall sconces struck vivid sparks from the jewels and glints from cloth of gold or silver.

The feast too, was unparalleled in Francesca's experience. As each dish was borne from the kitchen quarters by liveried footmen, to be served with expert flourishes by the stewards and set before the guests by deft servants, her eyes widened more and more. Was this how rich people lived? Course succeeded course, in a series of unimaginable dainties, clever kitchen conceits such as the whole swan roasted and refurbished in its shining white feathers, and exotic fruits such as she had never seen—all to be washed down with the smoothest of wine that cleared the palate for the next dish, to be savored in a hint of finest grapes.

Her eyes widened even farther, and in deep disapproval, at the amount of delicious food left on the plates. Francesca's thrifty peasant soul was shocked to its roots by guests who toyed with good meat, took no more than a few mouthfuls of the generous servings set before them and pushed away the plate . . . but she noticed no one refused the wine. Nor was any cup emptied as the wine steward passed along the tables offering refills!

For herself, she had firmly refused most of the dishes and sipped only one cup of wine. There was not only too much food; Francesca was of no heart to eat or enjoy.

After Gino and her father had been carried bruised and battered from the castle roof, Prince Prospero had escorted her trembling figure back to Juliana's bedchamber, completely ignoring her tearful pleas and protests. "Do not trouble your head about Juliana, my dear," he said finally, in the indulgent tone of a father. "You are a good child to speak in her favor, but it is no concern of yours. No," he raised his hand authoritatively as Francesca opened her mouth again, "not another word."

Perforce, Francesca had hung her head and walked along beside him in silence until he had thrown open the door to her room. "You will rest for a while, until the servants have poured your bath and robed you in the gown I wish you to wear." he said casually, raising her hand to his lips. "You are to be beautiful for me tonight," he finished, ushering her into the room and closing the door with a polite bow.

Francesca stumbled across the dim-lit room to fall on her knees beside the bed and pray as she had never prayed before in her life. She had dozed slightly, in the darkness of exhaustion, until two obsequious maids tapped upon the door and instantly bustled in with the great tub, to set before the fireplace where they swiftly built a roaring fire amid clucks of deep disapproval.

"Milady should have rung for a servant to mend the fire! Maria, bring the dressing gown . . . Lucia, light the tapers by the mirror. Will you come, milady? Oh, how cold your hands! Maria, pour a glass of wine!"

Numbly, Francesca allowed herself to be divested of her clothing and tenderly inserted into the bath. There was no doubt its warmth was welcome. As the serving women trotted about briskly, eyeing Prince Prospero's new favorite covertly and exchanging glances of surprise accompanied by telling shrugs, Francesca slid farther down into the perfumed water. Almost she would have fallen asleep again, but that strength and a clear head were vital. God alone knew what lay ahead for this night.

Francesca shivered violently, and Maria solicitously leaned over her. "Will you take a sip of the wine, milady?"

It might help, at that. Francesca silently accepted the fragile crystal goblet and felt the wine stinging its way down her throat. She drank only half the glass; reason dictated caution here when it came to wine. She'd had no more than a few glasses in all her life, and never anything so seductive as Prospero's cellars afforded.

"Will you dress now, milady?" Lucia enticed, holding up the gown for Francesca's inspection. It was embroidered cunningly with gold thread and a design of winking diamonds, pearls and emeralds.

Maria stood waiting with the warmed drying cloths, and Francesca sighed deeply. Now the terror was about to begin; no longer could she hide in the depths of the hip bath lapped with warm water and sustained by sips of good wine.

"It grows late, milady." Maria murmured urgently. What on earth ailed the silly fool, she wondered inwardly—but if Maria failed to get her dressed and down the stairs in time to suit his Highness, there'd be . . . penalties. Maria shuddered uncontrollably at the thought, for the least of them would be a severe beating at the hands of the chief steward, and the worst would be a command to share Hop-Toad's bed. "Milady," she begged, extending the cloths, and finally Francesca pulled herself erect and stepped from the tub, to be patted dry before the fire.

In silence, she stood while the servants rapidly clothed her in the finest linen undershifts, in silence, she sat obediently while they drew silk hose over her legs and inserted her feet into softest leather slippers with sparkling diamond buckles. "Will you stand, milady?"

Francesca stood, and the gown dropped over her head, slithered down to bare shoulders and bosom, fell in gracious folds about her legs. "May I dress your hair, milady?" Dully, she suffered herself to be led to the dressing table and sat, staring at the mirror with blind eyes, while Lucia brushed and combed, stuck a pin her and there, with a running commentary of flattery. "Such lovely thick hair, milady, and the beautiful color! Quite the most fashionable this season, I assure you. How fortunate you are, to be sure! So many ladies must wear wigs, and here your own hair is all that could be desired. See, Maria—the lustre, the waves—superb!"

Maria was unimpressed. "Make haste!" she hissed in an undertone. "He said ten o'clock, and it's near half after nine, already!"

Between them, the maids finished at top speed. Maria rubbed perfumed ointment over shoulders and breasts, touched her lips with salve . . . Lucia hung a magnificent necklace of diamonds and emeralds about her throat, and placed a matching ornament strategically among the soft waves of hair above her temples. Francesca sat sill, or stood, or turned and walked this way or that, as the maids directed.

"She seems entranced," Lucia muttered uneasily, but Maria only shrugged and whispered, "More like one of those marionettes in the show his Highness presented last year. Make haste!"

At long last: "Will you look milady?" With an effort, Francesca studied herself in the long mirror and noted the anxious faces of the two women.

"You have done a very good job," she told them, tonelessly, but as they smiled and sighed with relief, Francesca knew their worry. *Poor things,* she thought with detachment, *I wonder what he would do to them if I were displeased?*

Now Lucia had swung open the door, Maria had thrown a thin silk-tissue scarf about her shoulders and was gently pushing her forward. As she stepped into the corridor, the great clock in the lower hall began to strike the hour, and she was aware of the terrified whitening in the maid's faces. "Thank you," she said with a wan smile, "I shall tell his Highness how well you have cared for me, and that any delay is entirely my fault."

"Bless you, milady!" Maria muttered fervently, as Lucia added, obtusely, "May you enjoy the evening in your beauty, milady!"

Francesca's lips twisted sardonically, "Thank you." Steadily she went forward to the staircase and descended, while the clock tolled sonorously. At the foot of the steps Prince Prospero came through the curtains from the banquet hall and stood, looking up at her with appreciative eyes. Francesca forced herself to meet his eyes, forced herself to maintain her leisurely pace of dignity, and reached the step that brought her level with the Prince's tall figure exactly as the clock struck its final note.

Prospero smiled at her brilliantly, extending his hand. "You are a delight, milady," he remarked with genuine admiration. "You learn so quickly! A magnificent entrance!" He bent over her hand, brushing it with his lips as she stepped down the last paces . . .

And now at the beginning of the feast, Francesca sat beside the giver of that feast, holding herself together by sheer nerve.

They sat at one end of the main banquet table. At the other end, Juliana was clothed in a shimmering gown of ruby red, with Alfredo leaning intimately toward her. Francesca drew a tiny sigh of relief at sight of Juliana. So the Prince had not thrown her into a dungeon nor had her killed or something dreadful . . . at least, not yet. Her eyes flew toward Prospero, and met his dark gaze that held a gentle twinkle.

"Now I wonder why *will* you doubt me, my dear?" he murmured, patting her hand, while the first dinner plate was set before her. Staring at him, Francesca shook her head mutely, half-convinced once more of his essential kindliness. He smiled boradly, and turned away to gaze at the guests.

For some moments, she occupied herself with the meat on her plate, covertly copying his use of the unaccustomed knife and fork, and feeling rather proud of herself for mastering the art. She was, actually, *hungry,* and the roasted fowl was vaguely familiar despite the odd flavors of seasonings and sauce. Francesca cleaned her plate tidily, and took a sip of wine, as the plate was whisked away and replaced with a plate of meat. Unconsciously she frowned thoughtfully and inspected it with care. This was something she definitely failed to recognize.

Glancing sideways along the table, she noticed the Prince looking out over the assemblage with an urbane smile and his head cocked to one side judicially. For the first time, she realized there were four empty seats beyond him—and as he sensed her bewilderment, Prospero turned to smile at her. "You enjoyed the first dish," he remarked approvingly. "Good! Remind me to send a message to the cook, commending him for pleasing you."

"It was excellent," she said, politely.

"Arturo will be overjoyed to hear your praise," he murmured, "but you will like this even better, I feel certain."

Francesca looked at him squarely. "What is it?" she asked, boldly.

"Roasted wood boar," he said, and added drily, from the number of accomplished poachers in the late village of Estaban. I'm sure you must long since have grown accustomed to its flavor."

Francesca flushed hotly and glared at him. *"My* father was never among the poachers, you Highness!"

"No?" he raised an indolent eyebrow, and chuckled. "Then to you, this will be a novelty," he remarked softly, and under the teasing twinkle in his dark eyes, Francesca nearly capitulated into an answering chuckle—until memory struck coldly. *My father was never a poacher,* but for all that, he was below stairs awaiting who knew what unimaginable horror devised by this soft-spoken devil beside her?

Francesca stared blindly at her dinner plate, and Prospero's voice commanded, "Try it!" Awkwardly, she picked up the strange knife and fork, essayed to cut the meat, but already she'd lost the trick to it and the meat slid dangerously from one side to the other of the plate, threatening to land in her lap. Francesca bit her lip to control a sob of fright, and with a light laugh, Prospero's slender hands covered hers with a spring-steel strength, guiding her motions until the meat fell apart in neat sections.

Enclosed in his long arms, with his breath softly touching her cheek as he helped her cut the meat, Francesca cowered away from him, holding herself rigid against the hypnotic allurement of his suave strength. It would be so easy, so perilously easy, to relax, to sink back into the protection of those arms.

She set her lips firmly and raised her chin, until he brushed her bare shoulder with a fleeting kiss and removed his hands with a deep chuckle. "Thank you, your Highness," she said, formally, and out of her flash of private anger, murmured with mock humility, "What can a poor peasant girl know of these things, after all?"

The dark glance flicked over her. "Yes, yes," he drawled softly. "Decidedly, you are unusual—and as delightful as unexpected." Francesca's mouth trembled mutinously, but before she could reply, he said, "Eat your meat, child," and turned to look away over the tables crowded into the ballroom floor and thronged with guests growing more and more riotous.

In silence, Francesca sampled the meat. There was no doubt that it was delicious—but what were Gino and Ludovico eating in their cells? Sickened, she set down her fork, and the velvety voice beside her said, "Don't worry; they eat as well as you this night."

Startled, she whirled quickly, but Prospero was leaning back in his carved armchair, surveying the scene with a faint smile, as though his guest were merely so many pets—vicious pets, perhaps, but easily controlled for his amusement.

Slowly, she picked up the fork once more and ate the meat, very carefully, one piece at a time. When she had finished every piece, she realized hers was the only empty plate on the entire table!

She took a small sip of wine, and her glass was instantly refilled to the brim. The empty plate vanished, and a new dish sat before her; a small earthenware casserole, bubbling hot with a sauce that made her nose wrinkle unconsciously in a sniff of delight. This she recognized: the tiny shellfish called *langosta,* that once in a long while someone had brought from the sea that lay beyond the hills.

Francesca looked hopelessly at it, and Prospero's voice asked casually, "Something displeases you, milady?"

"No," she shook her head violently, "only—I ate too much already."

"Ah, a common disaster," the Prince murmured with suppressed amusement, "with more to follow, I fear. Arturo has obviously outdone himself this time. You may expect a dozen more dishes to follow, and," with a smiling glance at her slender figure, "if you insist upon cleaning your plate, I have not the faintest idea *where* you will put all the delicacies facing you. Francesca glanced about, at the loaded plates of food merely tasted and set aside, and firmed her lips, "I should *wish* to put them in the bellies of every starving peasant your Highness," she said, evenly.

Momentarily the dark eyes glared at her angrily, but Francesca tilted her chin and looked about casually, as though hers was the most normal of comments. He show of defiance was rewarded with a reluctant snort of laughter from Prospero, but it had taken too much of her inner strength. She sat pale and frightened as the Prince rose in his place.

"Hear me," he said, and soft as was his voice, the room fell silent in a twinkling. "Soon you will begin costuming yourselves for the Masque—a celebration of victory over death." His slender fingers toyed with various things laid before him on the table. Francesca's eyes slid sideways and widened in horror, while still she sat motionless.

The articles that had replaced Prospero's dinner plate were: *five delicate poignards.*

"Signor Scarlatti and his wife will not be joining us," he observed gently. "He fail to obey me . . ."

His hand flashed up and down . . . and one of the daggers quivered in the table before a vacant seat. There was a stifled gasp from one of the painted harlots at a lower table, then silence again throughout the hall, and Prospero picked up a second dagger, running it gently up and down his cheek, as he looked about at his guests.

"Yet because of me, you—unworthy though you may be—are safe from the Red Death. I promise you."

Again his hand flashed, and a knife quivered before the second empty chair, while Lampredi suppressed a nervous giggle.

"Unless, of course," Prospero remarked softly, "you incur my displeasure."

Almost listlessly, his hand rose, and planted another knife before the next empty chair—and while still it quivered in its position, he went on, "Some of you are guilty of acts against me . . ." The fourth knife found its home, while Juliana stared at the Prince, breathing hard.

"And all of you harbor thoughts," Prospero remarked, drily. "But no more!" Balancing the final poignard delicately in his fingers, Prospero narrowed his eyes and sent it flying to the exact center of the long banquet table. "And now," he said, pleasantly, "a small entertainment . . ."

The Prince half-turned his head with an infinitesimal gesture of one finger, while there was a rustle among the guests, turning to follow his gaze toward the farther doorway. It swung open, and a guard prodded Gino and Ludovico forward. Francesca closed her eyes faintly and clenched her hands together beneath the table napery. Then, aware that her reaction must only give glance at him, and gazed steadfastly at the two men walking toward her. She caught first her father's eye, then Gino's and put every particle of her heart into her glance, knowing from the answering flicker in their eyes that her message was understood.

Gathering her courage together, Francesca deliberately squared her shoulders and settled herself comfortably in her chair, making her face totally impassive—and from the corner of her eye caught a convulsive movement of anger in the slender fingers, holding the crystal wine glass. She felt a surge of reckless satisfaction as the delicate stem snapped in Prospero's grasp. To have so disappointed him at the outset was *good!* Francesca ignored the shattered glass, the red wine stain seeping across the tablecloth and held her eyes firmly, expressionlessly, on the approaching pair.

Inwardly, she knew it would not be possible to offer more than a temporary check to the man beside her. Already his hands were relaxed, holding a fresh crystal goblet in leisurely fingers. Without even looking, Francesca knew Prospero was smiling once more. Raising the wine glass, he gestured casually toward Gino and Ludovico.

"These two are Christians," he observed to the assembled guest. "They believe in a dead God, who preached 'Love thy neighbor.' Therefore, they will not fight one another to save one of their lives!"

The soft voice was venomous with sarcasm, and Francesca's heart sank, as he took a small sip of the wine and continued lazily, "So I've designed a plan where each can have the honor and glory of *saving* the other's life."

Setting down the goblet, his hand gestured swiftly toward the banquet table before Gino and Ludovico. "There are five daggers," said Prospero. "One is tipped with a poison that kills within five seconds. Each man in turn will cut himself on the forearm."

In dead silence, the guests leaned forward, looking with wide-eyed expectancy at the two peasants. Ludovico stared at the row of knives impassively, while Gino's glance at the Prince was contemptuous loathing.

"Well, will you not lay down your life for your brother?" Prospero taunted.

Swiftly, without comment, Ludovico picked up one of the knives and cut his forearm. Tossing the knife to the floor he faced Prince Prospero with calm dignity. Throughout the room there was silence among the guests, while the ticking of the clock swept over them majestically. "one-two-three-four-five," Prospero counted, and sat down with a slight shrug. "Not that time. Next!"

Steadily, Gino chose one of the knives and, his gaze never leaving the Prince, cut his own forearm and threw the knife to the floor. Again, the guests sat in tense silence as the clock ticked away the seconds, but it was still not the poisoned knife. Francesca was almost at the end of her tether, shaking violently inside even as she forced herself to maintain complete calm. Whatever happened, she would suffer a permanent loss. Tears welled slowly into her eyes, as her father reached forward steadily, possessed himself of the third knife and cut his forearm.

Now the tension had mounted to an unbearable pitch and beside Francesca, the Prince looked at the impassive pair with a grudging respect mingled with the beginnings of temper—because the spectacle was not going as he had anticipated. There had been no slightest reluctance from either of the men, and no frantic pleas from the beautiful girl by his side—hence no need for the various witty phrases Prospero might have used to draw mirth from his guests.

Now there were only two knives remaining. One assured death—but as Gino and Ludovico exchanged glances, it was obvious even to Prospero that each wondered not how to save *himself,* but how to save the other man for Francesca's sake. Half-angrily, Prospero leaned forward to position the remaining knives. "Five seconds," he said imperiously, and unhesitatingly Gino reached for one knife and slashed his arm for the second time—but even as the room breathlessly counted the ticking clock, Ludovico had seized the remaining knife and lunged across the table toward the Prince, repeating strongly, "Five seconds!"

Francesca caught her breath in a great sob, for swift as her father had been, Prospero was swifter and Ludovico was impaled upon his short sword. Gino moved forward, but was forcibly restrained by the two guards, while Francesca rose with a strangled cry, seeking to reach her father. Prospero's steely grip caught her, thrust her into her seat without a glance, while Hop-Toad swiftly moved in front of her to grasp her arms.

When she would have struggled with him, he held her tightly and shook his head. His face was full of sympathy and understanding, yet warned her to go no further when the Prince was in a rage—and that Prospero was furious was undeniable, despite his outward calm.

"The game wasn't played properly," he stated, "so both will die."

Francesca collapsed against the kindly arms of the dwarf, moaning. Hop-Toad held her gently maneuvering her back into her seat and shielding her from the curious eyes of the guests.

Gino stood squarely between the two guards and faced the

Prince. "You're a madman," he said contemptuously.

Prospero eyed him calmly. "Yet I will live and you will die," he remarked, his good humor suddenly restored. "Where is your God now in your time of need?"

"I shall see Him in Paradise," Gino returned, quietly.

"In the role of a martyr?" Prospero burst out laughing. "No. I will not have you killed. No glory for you my sturdy friend! No, indeed. I set you free."

There was an audible gasp through the banquet room, while Gino stared at him in disbelief. What new subtlety had this devil devised?

Francesca was more trusting. Hope springing in her heart, she started to turn thankfully toward the Prince, when his voice went on gently, "I set you free—free to go back to your village *and the Red Death.*"

Now she was terrified again. "No, I beg of you!" she cried, stretching forth a tentative hand.

Prospero sank into his chair beside her and took her hand softly in his. "I'm giving him a further 'glorious' chance to prove his faith," he told her ironically, and signed to the guards to remove Gino.

As they turned him roughly and began dragging him away, Francesca pulled her hand from Prospero's and sought to stand, but again Hop-Road restrained her with a meaning grimace. *"Not now!"* he mouthed and thrust her back into her chair.

At the doorway, Gino's voice came strongly over his shoulder. "Francesca, be of good heart. I'll come back for you, somehow . . ." Then he was hauled away through the door, and the music began to play.

Francesca turned to Prospero, who was calmly sipping his wine. "Let me go with him," she begged in an undertone. "Please!"

The dark eyes looked at her tenderly. "Impossible, my dear. No, I could not bear to think . . ." Fleetingly, his forefinger traced the curve of her cheek, and suddenly the moment was past. Springing to his feet, he addressed the guests. "To your rooms! Prepare for the masque! You are not to appear in costume until the stroke of midnight—and when the great clock strikes the final notes, then . . .ah, then!" Prospero lifted his wine glass elated, feverishly happy.

"Then will the revel of revels begin!" he cried and drained his glass, to throw it aside with a deep laugh.

In a sudden release from tension, the guests pushed back their chairs and prepared to depart. Some stood and raised their glasses in a final toast to the Prince; others babbled excitedly to each other and jostled slowly toward the main staircase, until at last there was only Prospero, lolling imperiously in his great chair with Francesca beside him.

Impulsively, she turned to him. "Bring Gino back and—I will do whatever you wish," she said in an undertone.

Prospero looked at her curiously. "You would destroy yourself for him?"

"Yes," she said simply.

He stared at her for a long moment. "You—cause me to doubt," he muttered finally—but as Francesca bent toward him, beseechingly, there was a voice behind them.

"Prospero," said Juliana deeply. "My Prince."

The Prince whipped about, almost with a breath of relief. Between the side curtains that his a door Francesca had not seen her before, Juliana stood with the dignity of a queen. "I am ready," she said, and extended her arms slowly.

"Your Highness," Francesca whispered shakily, but he ignored her. His face was illumined with sudden passion and he walked toward Juliana as though hypnotized.

"I am ready, too," he said softly, and turned her back through the hidden door without a glance for Francesca.

As the tapestries settled suavely into place across the closed door, Francesca sank into her chair and buried her face in her hands, sobbing uncontrollably. She had been so near, so very close, to receiving Prospero's permission to join Gino—and Juliana had defeated it. She had thought the older girl her ally, desiring as deeply to be rid of Francesca as Francesca wished to be rid of the castle—and yet, everything had been spoiled by Juliana. Almost, she could have cursed the girl . . .

"Milady, hush you! Come away, milady!" A hand tugged urgently at her sleeve, and through her tear-swollen eyes Francesca raised her head to face the ugly visage of Hop-Toad. Behind him a bevy of servants scurried to clear away tables, to tidy and ready the room for the midnight revel. "Lean on me," the dwarf said with gentle dignity. "Let me help you to your chamber, milady."

Tremulously, Francesca smiled at him—the ghost of a smile, but a sincere response to the genuine sympathy in his eyes. "Yes," she whispered, exhaustedly. "Oh, you are kind! You understand, don't you?"

"Better than anyone, milady," he said, pulling her from her chair and placing her hand to lean on his twisted shoulder. "Come away, now, and be of good cheer, milady, for your man *will* return. Never doubt it! Mind the step here . . . Oh, he's a brave fellow, he'll best Prince Prospero yet, you'll see . . ."

Somehow Francesca found herself at her bedchamber door, facing the dwarf who came only to her waist. "They call you Hop-Toad, but that isn't your real name, is it?"

"I was christened Ernesto," he admitted.

"It's a nice name," she said. "It fits you. Thank you for taking care of me, Ernesto." She held out her hand with a smile.

"It was my pleasure, milady," he told her, drawing himself erect as possible and kissing her hand with as much graceful courtesy as Prospero himself. Stepping back, he grinned at her encouragingly. "And mind what I said! That man of yours'll be back to get you. Don't you fret, but rest a while and leave it to him! He sketched a salute, bowed deeply, and swaggered away down the corridor, while Francesca went into her chamber with a half-smile touching her lips. What a good-hearted little man he was!

Below stairs the great clock began to strike. Francesca unconsciously counted as she let the door fall closed behind her and went wearily across to sink into the fireside chair. Eleven of the clock, and an hour before the promised masquerade. She had planned no costume. While the other guests had rummaged in the great wardrobes, she had been trying to rescue Gino and her father—and now her father was dead and Gino was being thrust beyond the castle walls to die of the Red Death.

Francesca twisted in her chair and wept uncontrollably, heedless of the damage to tear stains on her gorgeous white gown, where was Ludovico's body . . . *and where was Gino?*

Chapter IX

GINO was free.

Once withdrawn from the banquet hall, the guards had driven him ahead of them like an animal, whacking him viciously with the flat of their swords, although taking care not to slash him mortally. His Highness had definitely stated the peasant pig was not to be killed within the castle, but to be thrust out to die of the Red Death. On the other hand, there was the matter of Louis, and Bertrand, and Guglielmo—all dead because of this lout. Impossible to resist a few extra whacks in honor of their dead companions.

"Don't hit him on the head!" Josef said authoritatively. "Sometimes they die unexpectedly. Go for the shoulders and legs . . ."

He fell three times getting across the outer courtyard, but he had still the strength to get to the portcullis, where Luigi had been ruthlessly roused by an advance guard to release the chains of the drawbridge and pull up the gate, far enough for the guards to seize Gino bodily and literally heave him across to the outer dirt road.

As he rolled breathlessly, groggily, to his feet and glared back across the bridge to the threatening guardsmen, Gino steadied himself. "To hell with all of you!" he said with deadly clarity. Turning on his heel, he ran swiftly into the moonlit night, while the guards laughed uproariously behind him.

Peering after the figure disappearing into the shadows of the road toward Estaban, Josef said, "Pull up the bridge, Luigi. He's gone to his death, the fool—and the rest of us will live!" Turning back to the courtyard while Luigi once more sealed the castle, Josef strolled toward the guard room.

"All the same, I think he got away too easily," Marco observed with a scowl. "Louis, Bertrand, Guglielmo—that's a score that should have been settled."

"The Red Death will settle it better than anything we have here," Josef told him with a laugh. "Come on—I'm for a cup of wine and a bit of meat before we go on duty for the Masque. Who's with me?"

"I'm with you—and I, Josef . . . A good suggestion," the guards chorused heartily, trooping after him. There was no doubt in any-one's mind, now Bertrand was dead, that Josef would be the captain of the palace guard. Neither did anyone have any reservations about it. Bertrand had been a good captain. He'd been just, fair in portion-ing duties, not unduly strict, but there was no denying Josef . . .

Well, it'd be a different guard room once he took over! There'd be an eye winked for a guard delayed in going on duty because of romantic involvements—and there'd be all the wine Josef could wheedle out of the Prince, extra rations of meat, a ducat here and a ducat there for duties well carried out.

Oh, Josef was a famous fellow, no doubt about it! Slapping each other on the back, the guards swaggered back to the courtyard door leading down to the guard room.

Beyond the first curve in the road, with the castle hidden from sight, Gino slowed to a walk, breathing heavily and limping a little from the vicious bruises inflicted by the guards. About him were only skeleton trees, denuded of leaves, with bare arms waving fantastically in the cold winds of early winter. Involuntarily, Gino shivered in his tattered jerkin. Clapping himself briskly across the chest, he went along to the next curve in the road down to Estaban, and here he could once more survey the lighted menace of the castle.

Tight-lipped, he studied what he had escaped. The castle seemed surrounded by noxious mists, through which its lights were half-hidden, beaming out as the fog drifted, only to be veiled again. Momentarily Gino paused, twisting his hands together in anguish. Somewhere within those dread walls was Francesca, whom he had promised to rescue. Ahead of him lay—nothing. From the conversation of the guards, Gino had no doubt of this. His cottage, his parents, friends, neighbors: all were gone by order of his Highness.

Still, Gino went steadily on. He must see for himself what had become of the people of Estaban. Perhaps there would yet be time to rebuild before full winter, and strong hands would be needed. A day or two of rest, to recover from the bruises, and Gino'd be fit as ever, able to help whoever remained.

Behind him there was the scream of a woman in pain, floating dimly down from the castle. Gino froze, and whirled around as the scream sounded again. *Francesca,* he thought, agonized, but for a moment there was only silence. Then in the bare branches of the trees above him there was a rustling. Gino started involuntarily and stared upward—at a hunting owl swooping in a long arc past him to pounce on a field mouse.

He gulped, and tried to steady his pounding heart. Only an owl. How many times he'd seen them in the fields about Estaban, nothing to be frightened of, only an owl searching for an unwary field mouse . . . Gino went on, quickening his pace unconsciously, and fighting down terror of the country around him. So familiar in sunlight, it was somehow oddly threatening and unknown in the pallid moonlight.

Above him the dry tree branches rattled like skeletons, while on every side the underbrush assumed grotesque shapes and forms. The wind sighed and moaned around his ears, cutting cruelly through the torn jerkin. After everything Gino had endured in the last twenty-four hours, his native common sense was faltering, and when there was a strange cry from one of the trees, he stopped dead to stare upward.

Twin red sparks flashed angrily at him from a tree limb—and another scream.

A wildcat. . . .

Gino surrendered to panic and took to his heels, bolting pell-mell down the road until his chest was near to bursting for lack of breath and he could go no farther. Swerving drunkenly away from the road, he collapsed onto the ground, crawling into the shadows of the sparse undergrowth and gasping for breath. For a long while he lay on the barren ground, trying to compose himself. At last he was able to sit up, wrapping his arms about his knees and shivering in the cold air.

Looking about him, he knew where he was: on the hillside just before the entrance to the village of Estaban—but there was no more Estaban. Where there should, even at this late hour of night, have been some glimmering of banked hearth fires flickering through cottage windows here and there, was only a black and empty wasteland and the sour smell of dead fire. Gino clenched his hands together and felt a lump in his throat. He bent his head to his knees with a dry sob of despair—for where was he to go, what was he to do, how was he to survive until he could return for Francesca?

In his exhaustion, Gino was conscious of an alien sound that was not of hunting animals nor tree branches in the wind, but the soft snap of playing cards—reminiscent of the guard room games at the castle. Wildly, Gino's head rose and he stared about him, reconnoitering cautiously as any animal.

Clear in the moonlight bathing the top of the hill was the great tree—and beneath it a hooded figure leaned casually against the massive trunk. Gino recoiled, and a voice said, "My son!"

For a second, Gino hesitated, but there had been a warmth and affection in the voice that drew him. Slowly, wearily, Gino moved toward the shrouded figure, almost crawling on hands and knees, dragging himself upward until at last he settled himself nearby—and realized old Concetta had been right after all!

This must be the holy man she had met, in this same spot, and now Gino could see the glowing ruby red of his monk's habit, and the fine thin white fingers laying out the cards so deliberately in the moonlight.

"Tell me of it," the deep voice commanded calmly, and somehow Gino felt comforted, as though all things were possible, everything could be told.

Twisting onto his knees, he buried his face in his hands and cried out, anguished, "My God, my God . . ."

"Who is your God?"

"The true one, the only God," Gino said, bewildered.

"Yes," said the monk, with a note half-humorous and half-resigned in his tone. "Go on, tell me."

"I have sinned," Gino muttered, clasping his hands together and pressing them to his forehead. "I have—killed . . ."

"For yourself?" the monk inquired softly.

"No," Gino said thoughtfully after a moment. The monk raised his hand as though in blessing, and resumed his card game. "But now I'm afraid," Gino admitted. "Afraid!"

"For yourself?"

"For Francesca," Gino said, and added honestly, "and for me. I must return for her, and I don't know how. What weapon can I find against Prince Prospero!

"Had you thought of—love?" the man in red inquired lightly.

"In the air, through the trees, I found myself loving only myself and my own freedom," Gino said tonelessly. "I'm afraid of the town where the Red Death stalks . . . afraid of the castle where Prospero lurks." He pounded his hands together softly. "Afraid—afraid!"

"I give you a sign, my son," and the thin fingers extended a single playing card. Hesitantly, Gino took it and examined it. He thought it was an ace of hearts.

"What does it mean?"

"Mankind," the man in red told him, calmly continuing his card game, "and the only talisman you will need for the rest of your life. Look at it when you can . . . think of it always . . . and never fear it will open every door to your forever."

Gino held the card in his hands and stared at it blankly. How could a playing card help him to rescue Francesca from the castle? Yet somehow as he stared at the graceful heart in the center of the card, he felt conscious of new strength and determination. There would be a way; he would find it.

In the peaceful stillness of the hillside, Gino sat quietly behind the man in red, thinking as best he could. He was suddenly aware of distant chanting, a slender thread of beautiful melody. Involuntarily, Gino scrambled to his feet and turned toward the sound.

Winding through the valley road below him was a procession of tiny flames, stretching up the hill toward the castle. Frowning, Gino peered down at the dim cortege and took a few steps forward. Behind him, he could hear the soft snap of the card game. "I think I should go," he said hurriedly, over his shoulder, "but I thank you, father—and as soon as the village is rebuilt and I have Francesca with me, you will ever be welcome in our house."

"A handsome offer," the deep voice remarked with gentle amusement. "Thank you, my son—and good fortune attend you."

Gino only half heard his words. Clutching the card in his hands, he hurried down the hillside on a line to intersect the procession, but it had already nearly passed before he reached the road. Briefly, he paused in horror as the significance of the cortege permeated his mind: before him wound the remains of Estaban in a parade of death, and it was far worse than he had dreamed.

In the forefront strode Rodolpho, the village elder carrying a lantern in his hand. Behind him, four of the surviving inhabitants carried a plank on which lay a covered body. They were followed by two men, an old woman, and a small child, carrying lighted candles, and bringing up the rear was a farm cart piled high with the dead bodies of the villagers, and driven by an old man.

The procession was nearly gone into the darkness of the winding road to the castle before Gino came to himself and ran after it—to lift the shroud from the figure on the plank. "Anselmo!" Replacing the covering, Gino ran this way and that, trying to identify any familiar face and shuddering at the recognitions in the final cart of heaped bodies. "Marguerita, Elizabetta—Roberto, Ruggiero—no!"

Frantically, he stumbled down the length of the cortege to Rodolpho and grasped his arm. "Where do you go? The burial ground is only beyond the hill."

"We go to the castle."

"Why?"

"To beg forgiveness of the Prince," Rodolpho told him, dully.

"Forgiveness!" Gino was beside himself with rage. "For what?"

"For however we have sinned."

"No!" Gino protested wildly. "You go to beg at the house of Satan himself. *No,* I tell you!"

"Better that than the Red Death," Rodolpho said flatly, shaking himself free as Gino tried to halt him.

"Stop," he implored hoarsely. "You do not know what you do!"

"It is all we have left to do," Rodolpho told him, and pushed Gino away, so that he stumbled and fell in the dirt of the roadside. The cortege made its way forward and was shortly lost to sight around the next curve.

Gino lay still in the moonlight and felt tears of mingled despair and rage in his eyes. *The fools, the silly blind fools,* he raged inwardly, and there was no way to stop them. Panting exhaustedly, he was conscious now of his aching bruised body . . . and something else.

His hand still clutched the playing card. What had the man in red called it? "I give you a sign, its meaning is Mankind." Gino peered at his talisman, carefully smoothing out the creases from his clenched fingers, and once more he felt strangely hopeful. Courage returned in a flow through his bones. Holding the card in both hands, he sat up. *I will rest a while,* he thought, *and then I will return to the castle . . .*

Within every chamber guest arrayed themselves for the masque. Hop-Toad was already disguised as an African pygmy, his skin covered with dark paint upon which white streaks crossed his cheeks, giving him a fearsome aspect. In Alfredo's room he was assisting the Duke into the ape's skin from Prospero's storeroom.

"Won't this thing get uncomfortably hot?" Alfredo asked, irritably.

"It may become a trifle warm," Hop-Toad said soothingly, "but it won't be for long."

The Duke paused, half in and half out of the costume, and eyed the dwarf dubiously.

"After the unmasking you can take it off," Hop-Toad pointed out, "because the game will be over."

"True enough," Alfredo agreed. "All right. Get on with it."

Hop-Toad finished fastening up the back, and picked up the head. "See, the eyes are of crystal, you'll be able to see everything. Just bend your head a bit farther this way, Duke . . . that's right. There we are!" Hop-Toad said cheerfully, fitting the head in place and adjusting it carefully. "You can see clearly?" Alfredo muttered a muffled assent. "Perfect! Now—see yourself!" Hop-Toad turned him toward the wall mirror, and Alfredo shambled over, his movements made awkward by the legs of the costume.

"Now crouch low and swing your arms," the dwarf suggested, and Alfredo obediently essayed his role. Bending down, he swung his arms back and forth, touched the knuckles of one hand to the floor and took a few ungainly leaps to one side and the other. Straightening up, he grunted realistically and beat his chest. Suddenly, the Duke was thoroughly into the spirit of the game, and began to roar with laughter, as he practiced shambling and waving his arms threateningly.

Hop-Toad guffawed appreciatively. "Oh, excellent! What a sensation you'll be!" Taking a small whip from his belt, the dwarf pretended to strike Alfredo with it, roaring, "Back, mighty animal! I am your keeper brought from deepest Africa to control your strength."

The Duke pretended to make a grab, snarling, while Hop-Toad nimbly leaped aside and continued the burlesque, alternatively flourishing the absurd little whip and pretending he was scared out of his wits, until Alfredo was so overcome with laughter, he couldn't go on. Falling on the floor, he gasped delightedly. "Wait till I catch my breath, and we'll practice some more. Oh you're a clever fellow. Who'll ever think *I* am the great big ape . . ."

"Who, indeed?" Hop-Toad agreed blandly.

Within the black door, Juliana knelt trembling at the altar, chanting strange words rhythmically. Hesitantly, she reached forward to lift an intricately chased silver cup, and as she brought it toward her, it began to steam furiously. With a swift motion, Juliana set it to her lips and drank . . . only to cast away the cup clattering beside the altar and clutch her throat with both hands as the boiling liquid burned its way down her gullet.

Coughing and choking desperately, she closed her eyes in pain—but now it was almost done, almost over. Only a few moments more of agony, she thought vaguely, and Prospero would be hers forever. Already the pain was less, and slowly she began to open her eyes, for now—*now*—she was about to see the vision, to receive the sign.

Suddenly the blood-red window behind the altar blazed forth a stream of harsh white light, in which Juliana was pin-pointed. Staring directly into the beam of light, she was paralyzed with fear—and aware of figures approaching from the darkness beyond the altar. All about her was a barbaric chant that increased steadily as the figures passed through the path of light and disappeared into the farther darkness to the left of the altar.

First, an Aztec priest with the obsidian knife of human sacrifice held in both hands, point downward before him. He was followed by a dread priest of Kali, with hair plastered in long greasy strands around a face ashen-gray. His hands held a rippling Kris, and the many armed effigy of black, bloody-tongued Kali hung about his neck. As he passed through the light he paused and faced Juliana briefly—and all Kali's arms moved snake-like, writhing, beckoning . . .

Then he was gone, and a Druid priest in a blood-stained white robe stepped into the light, but even as Juliana's starting eyes beheld him, he was gone, to be succeeded by a gigantic African witch doctor. His neck was encircled by a clattering necklace of bleached human skulls, and his height was increased by a feathered headdress above a frightful grinning mask of Death.

Juliana sobbed involuntarily and closed her eyes, while she felt rather than saw that the great beam of white light had vanished. "My Master Satan," she whispered pleadingly, and turned toward the throne chair beyond the altar. Once more bathed only in the blood-red light of the window, it seemed a shadowy figure sat there. Was it an immense bat, or perhaps a demon? Juliana caught her breath: could it be the Master himself?

Behind her was soft laughter, and whirling she stared into the darkness. "Prospero?" But there was only the laughter, and she sprang to her feet, moving toward the deepest shadows. "I am betrothed of the Devil," she said proudly. "I have seen the terrors."

"Not all of them," Prospero's voice was gently amused and a door slammed violently.

Juliana ran to the black door and threw it open wildly. "I survived my own sacrifice," she said defiantly, but the voice said only, "There is more . . . more . . .more."

"Prospero," she cried, "where are you?" There was no reply, but the soft click of a door shutting. Now she ran across the White Room, into the Purple Room beyond, to stand panting. "I am stronger in the Devil's favor than you," she almost screamed in the empty room, and went swiftly on to the Yellow Room, hearing the amused laughter taunting her.

Forcing herself to calmness, Juliana stood in the center of the room and said, "Together, on Earth, we will live as man and wife, and when He calls us, you shall be Satan and I still your wife." Steadily, she went to the last door and emerged into the marble-floored great hall. "I have tasted the beauties of terror."

"Hush," Prospero's voice told her soothingly, as she paused before the great ticking clock. "Listen . . . The passing of time, the beating of a heart, the footstep of an assassin." His voice (if it was his voice and not merely part of her vision, for where was he?) died away, and Juliana looked at the scimitar-shaped pendulum that swung to and fro, inexorably, hypnotically, glistening cruelly in the flickering candlelight.

"Destiny," Prospero's voice breathed—and the glass front of the tall clock case shattered before her face.

Involuntarily, Juliana screamed piercingly, and threw her hands to her ears with a second scream—and before her terrified eyes, it seemed the scimitar-pendulum swung forward in a wide arc that slashed again and again across her breast, until she fell to the marble floor. As the great clock began sonorously to toll midnight, Juliana lay unhearing in the stillness of death. Welling up through the torn bosom of her white gown, her heart's blood embroidered a pattern of red against which the dressmaker's design of diamonds sparkled with an additional fire.

Above stairs, the guests in their various costumes had poured from their rooms at the sound of Juliana's screams. They crowded to the top of the staircase, leaning over in a mixture of reactions. Some were aghast, others were expressionless. Alfredo's eyes narrowed and a faint smile touched his lips; Juliana, he recalled, had often been insolent to him. With a shrug, he went back to his chamber where Hop-Toad waited to help him don the ape's costume over his court evening dress . . .

In the muted whispering among the guests above, the deep clock chime continued to announce the hour. From the door to the Yellow Room, Prince Prospero walked across the floor, to look down at Juliana. He was impeccably dressed, but without his jacket. Looking up at the assembled guests, he said smoothly, "Do not mourn Juliana. She has just married a good friend of mine."

The final stroke, and the clock was once more silent, merely ticking evenly within the shattered glass of its case. The Prince turned away. "Now it is full midnight," he said jubilantly. "Let the masque begin!"

Within the great hall, music started as Prospero pulled aside the draperies, revealing the brilliantly lit room. Behind him the guests began descending the staircase with rising spirits, while averting their eyes from Juliana's dead body. There were a few who hurried past with a gulp, but once within the ballroom where servants were offering filled wine cups and the music was sprightly, they quickly put aside unpleasant matters and abandoned themselves to the dance sets forming in the center of the floor.

Prospero had disappeared once more, but momentarily he was not missed in the amusement of trying to guess which person was behind which mask. The dancing grew swifter in pace, the laughter rose to gale force as the wine circulated freely, and already a few masked couples were seeking the privacy of other rooms in which to conduct a more particular guessing game . . .

No matter what lay outside, within was only warmth and pleasure.

Gino and Ludivico face death through poison knives.

Jane Asher and David Weston

Chapter X

"WHAT'S THAT LIGHT?" A guard leaned over the parapet and peered intently down the road to Estaban. Over his shoulder he said to his companion on sentry duty, "Send for Josef! There's something queer going on."

To Gino it was equally queer—strange that not one of the dreary procession would listen to him, Gino, who'd actually been in one of the castle cells. After resting a while, he felt strong enough to follow with vigorous strides that shortly brought him alongside Rodolpho and the rest of the cortege again. Desperately, he had pleaded, using every argument he could think of.

"I am your friend. How long have you known me, Rodolpho? Since I was born! Did ever I lie to you? With your own eyes you saw me driven away from the village yesterday by the castle guards. Can you doubt my word that I was thrown into a cell, that Ludovico is dead from Prospero's sward thrust, that Francesca is still a prisoner in his foul hands?"

Rodolpho only shook his head and plodded forward. "No, I do not doubt you lad," he said, "but mine is the responsibility for what is left of the village—and it belongs to Prince Prospero, whether we will or no. I know not how we displeased him, but pride is not for such as we.

Helplessly, hopelessly, Gino fell back along the line and tried to dissuade one after another of the living villagers in the procession. They would not listen. In their various ways, they told him exactly what Rodolpho had said: We belong to the Prince, he does as he pleases with us, from him we must beg mercy.

Silenced at last, Gino could only accompany them along the upward curving road. The playing card was thrust within his ragged jerkin and lay against his heart. Once in a while, he reached to finger it gently, and it seemed he was comfortably warm despite the cutting chill of winter winds as they came out beyond the trees into unprotected land.

At last they rounded the final curve in the road, with Rodolpho tinkling the small death bell and raising his lantern high. About him, the remaining villagers stood abject and beaten. Gino stared up at the grim stones of the castle, and in the silence heard dim strains of gay music. *The masque,* he remembered with a shudder. Francesca would be there, beautifully gowned beside the Prince . . . Rapidly, Gino moved aside from the pitiful group at the moat, opposite the great drawbridge that was sealing the castle.

Rodolpho tinkled his bell again and swung the lantern back and forth. From the battlements above, a strong voice cried, "Who are you?"

"All that is left of the village of Estaban," Rodolpho said.

Staring up, Gino could dimly recognize the guard named Josef, in the plumed helmet that was formerly worn by Bertrand—but he, Gino, had killed Bertrand. Beside Josef, there was an archer.

"Estaban?" said Josef contemptuously. "Go back to it."

"We beg mercy of the Lord Prince Prospero!" Rodolpho pleaded, and Josef hesitated for a moment, then turned to the archer.

His voice came clearly through the night air. "Inform the Prince. It might amuse him."

As the archer vanished, Gino could not restrain a final plea. "Don't grovel before him and let him delight in the destruction of your souls, Rodolpho."

"I wish to save our bodies—those few that are left to us."

"Do you expect *any* plea to move his heart?" Gino cried. "If you must die, do it like human beings."

"You have not seen the Red Death, Gino," Rodolpho countered, dully.

"And you have not seen the dungeons of Prospero, nor his amusing games for entertaining his guests," Gino returned softly—but he knew it was useless.

With a sigh of defeat, he retreated toward the shadows of a small grove of trees. As he walked along, he took a final glance at the stolid faces of these people who had once been his friends and neighbors, even childhood playmates, and who now refused to meet his eyes. *Doomed,* he though, *all doomed* . . . and faced the small child whose taper had gone out, who stood shivering in his rags, understanding nothing of the scene about him.

Swiftly, Gino bent to pick the boy up and the child squealed in fright. "Shhh, don't be afraid, it's only Gino . . ." but even as the child leaned against his shoulder and relaxed, a powerful hand grasped Gino's wrist firmly.

"This is my child," the villager said in a tone that brooked no argument. "I must give him every chance, Gino. Let go!"

With a sob, Gino surrendered the child and ran away to the shadows of the trees. On the battlements above, Josef leaned forward sharply, while an archer beside him shouted tauntingly, "Where does the rabbit run?"

"That one fears Prospero far more than the Red Death," Josef remarked sardonically. "If I mistake not, he's the peasant pig we threw across the drawbridge an hour ago!"

"What's he doing, coming back here, in that case?" the archer asked in bewilderment.

Josef shrugged lightly. "With death and destruction, malice and venom, in his heart," he said casually. "His peasant sweetheart is within—under the personal protection of our Prince. *Very* personal," he added warningly, as the archers and guards snickered nastily.

"You mean there's a female in the castle you haven't sampled?" one guard tittered.

"Everything in good time," Josef said languidly, and sprang to attention. "His Highness approaches . . ."

Instantly all the archers and guards drew themselves up rigidly, as Prince Prospero stepped onto the castle roof and walked across the parapet, ignoring the sentries. Leaning over, he surveyed the dismal group before him. "What do you want?" he called out, annoyed.

"Mercy, great Prince!" Rodolpho begged. "This is all that is left of us in Estaban. The winter comes on a freezing wind. We are without shelter . . ."

"Dig a burrow as the fox and hare do."

"The wells and streams will be frozen, and there is no food," Rodolpho said.

"Store up nuts like the squirrels," Prospero returned, impatiently, and behind him the archers laughed sycophantically.

"Mercy!" roared at the top of his lungs, and fell to his knees, followed by all the living villagers extending praying hands. "Give us the sanctuary of the castle walls."

"Give *me* an end to your pleading," Prospero said, "and go back where you came from."

"We will die!"

"If you refuse to go," the Prince's voice was final, "then—die here. Archers . . ."

Quickly the men sprang forward in a line, to raise the crossbows and set the bolts, while Prospero stepped back a pace and spoke to Josef. "Not the child."

"It will perish anyway," Josef said involuntarily, astonished.

"*Not* the child," the Prince stated, and it was a command.

"Yes, your Highness," Josef murmured, and signalled to the archers. "You heard the Prince? *Not* the child . . ."

Without a backward glance, Prospero went away to the door in the battlements and down the stairs. As he descended, leisurely, his ears caught the singing whine of the arrows, and for a moment his finely-chiselled lips twisted sadly. "Why did they force me to be harsh?" he mused with a sigh. Faintly he heard a second charge of arrows, and his shoulders drooped. "The child will die, of course, as Josef said," he shook his head slightly, and straightened the fall of gold lace over his wrist with a deft finger. "A pity I have such a tender heart . . ."

At the head of the main staircase, he encountered two liveried footmen holding plaited rush baskets. "Ah, yes, I had all but forgotten," Prospero drawled. "Follow me." He went along the bedroom corridor and knocked imperiously upon Francesca's door, which was immediately opened by Lucia, curtseying deeply. "Milady is ready?" Prospero inquired politely.

"Yes, certainly, your Highness!" Maria babbled, pulling Francesca to her feet ruthlessly and shoving her forward as quickly as possible.

The Prince surveyed her shimmering azure gown embroidered in pearls and diamonds . . . the necklace of huge sapphires set with diamonds that sparkled above her bosom, the twinkling diamond-tipped pins that fastened her hair in lustrous waves . . . down to the dainty sky-blue leather slippers encrusted with diamonds and finished with gay little silver tassels that swayed and danced as Francesca came toward him. "Very nice," he said, and extended a hand while Maria went weak at the knees from relief.

Numbly, Francesca laid her hand in Prospero's and suffered herself to be led farther along the corridor to a doorway from which curtains were swiftly withdrawn, admitting them to a gallery overlooking the great hall and revelry below.

Prospero moved forward holding Francesca beside him, and turning to the two footmen who had lined up on his other hand. Idly, his slender fingers grasped a handful of *something* within the first basket. "Gifts for everyone," his deep voice cut across the music, and his hand flew out in a graceful circular gesture.

"Rubies, pearls, emeralds," he said casually, and again his hand scattered jewels gleaming in a rainbow of colors over the throng below. "Gifts for my guest—for my friends," and as the people wildly knelt to the floor and scrambled for the precious stones, Prospero took first one basket, then the other, from the impassive footmen and emptied them with a final toss that sent a spray of sparkles to the farthest corners of the room.

Below was pandemonium, chaos, a positive fracas between several of the women fighting each other for possession of a particularly good jewel. Prospero laughed uproariously. "Look at them," he said to Francesca. "Scrambling like starving men for crusts of bread. They're all wealthy—yet all greedy for more."

Francesca stood in silence; to her peasant mind, the scene below resembled nothing so much as a barnyard group of sows and hogs jockeying for position at the swill trough. At her side, the Prince saw nothing wrong with it. As Anna-Marie and Signora Escobar came to blows over an inch-square emerald, he threw back his head and laughed with more genuine enjoyment than Francesca had ever heard from him.

"Look at them!" He grasped her arm and hugged it, while his eyes were still fixed on the struggling women below. "Hi-yi, Anna-Marie almost got it that time—but watch the Escobar's riposte! A formidable woman, I promise you . . . ha, there! A definite hit, look at Anna-Marie rolling over, but she's only feinting, I assure you." Prospero chuckled, and as Anna-Marie secured the priceless gem with a well-calculated snatch and scuttled away behind the concealing cloaks and dominos of the masquers' costumes while

Signora Escobar screamed abuse after her, the Prince was nearly in tears of laughter.

Francesca stood silently beside him, lost in the lethargy of nightmare, but Prospero was oblivious. When he could control himself, he stepped forward to the gallery railing and raised his arms. "I give you reason for real rejoicing," he said strongly, his voice ringing out across the room below and creating instant silence. "Hear me!" Swiftly, the guests turned to look up at his commanding figure expectantly.

"The only survivors of the village of Estaban came to the castle walls this night. There were only a dozen," he said casually. "The Red Death has claimed all the rest—but as I promised you, all within these walls and under my protection are safe. So rejoice!"

There was a chorus of happy cries, a few faint cheers, from the guests below, and once more the orchestra began the dance music. The dancers formed the sets and stepped with even more joyous abandon—for were they not alive while all else beyond the castle walls was dead or threatened with death?

As Prospero glanced happily over the throng, Francesca came out of her lethargy and touched his sleeve timidly. He turned to smile down at her. "Yes, milady?"

"Those who live?" she whispered fearfully.

"No longer," he told her, not without sympathy. "They demanded entry to the castle."

"And—you killed them?

"It was a kindness, my dear," he said, taking her hand warmly in both of his. "Can't you see that? The Red Death brings pain, madness, horror—and I spared them all of that." Pulling her hand up to his lips, he murmured, "After the masque tonight, I will initiate you into understanding. There are worse things than death, my dear."

She moved away from him, shaking her head wearily. "I don't know, perhaps you are right," she remarked with a flash of spirit. "But I was one of Estaban, and if you killed the others—why not me?"

Prospero smiled at her appreciatively. "Glorious!" he remarked, cocking his head to one side judicially. "There is just that certain touch of individuality about you, milady, that was lacking in—all the others." He came forward, smiling, to draw her hand within his arm and lead her away through the draperies from the gallery. "No," he said softly, "I have other plans for you, my dear. Shall we return to the dance?"

Upon the battlements, the fun was over. With one comprehensive glance at the desolation beyond the moat, Josef said, "Well done lads. You got all of them except that lout who ran away—but no matter where he runs, the Red Death will claim him. Let's away to the guard room for a cup of wine, eh?"

Jovially, they went down the long staircase, past the shattered clock and the sounds of revelry from the ballroom, down again to the lower level where they cast the dice to decide who would toil up to the battlement again with a cup of wine for Guiseppe, standing sentry alone in the cold winter wind. It was Josef's idea, and even when Marco was the loser and went off with a groan, there was no doubt that only Josef would have remembered the comrade on duty. Unquestionably, the guard room was going to be easier and more comfortable from now on, and when Marco finally came puffing back down the stairs, it was Josef who made much of his noble effort and swiftly had him in a jolly mood again.

Hidden in the wood shadows, Gino shuddered with nausea as the remnants of Estaban were felled by Prospero's archers. In the still night air, his keen ears caught the interchange of words on the battlements, followed by silence. Still he waited cautiously; there would be at least one guard left as sentry. Sure enough, after a while there were footsteps and a hearty thanks for the cup of wine . . . a few bluff words exchanged, and again retreating steps.

Looking out toward the moat, Gino could see Rodolpho's lantern overturned, yet still flickering on the ground. A small figure sobbed hysterically, huddling over one of the slain villagers: the child Prospero had commanded the bowmen to spare. Gino crawled forward on his belly, slowly reconnoitering. If he could only determine when the guard had gone around to the other side of the battlements, he could rescue the child at least, but if he misjudged the moment, any slightest movement would bring an instant arrow from the guard.

Never had Gino listened more thoughtfully, for the minute sounds of leather boots, the faint click of metal, the smallest indication of the guard's routine on the heights above. He pulled himself inch by inch to the absolute edge of the shadows, and deliberately waited. Once—twice—he heard the guard walking away, pacing into silence and returning, and his peasant sense of time clocked the rhythm of the sentry-go.

It would be necessary to race out to the child, to lie motionless among the dead bodies for the space of one tour of duty; then to pick up the child and race back to the concealment of the trees. It was going to be a tricky thing, but Gino thought he could do it. Once the child was secure, he would carry out the plan that had occurred to him for re-entering the castle.

Crouching in runner's position, Gino could hear the taint tap of the guard's paces retreating. Instantly he was rearing across to cast himself panting beside the desolate little figure. "Don't make a sound," he breathed warningly, "don't be afraid, it's only Gino."

With a slight scream, the child threw himself at Gino, crying, "Gino, Gino take me away, I'm scared . . ."

Gino could hear the guard's footsteps returning quickly. Evidently he'd heard the child's voice and was coming to investigate. Gino pulled the child into his arms, half-smothering it and hissing, "Lie *very* still, pretend I'm dead, too—or the guard will shoot me!" It was an agonizing pretence, in which Gino lay motionless among his dead friends, while the boy quivered and sobbed above him, but at long last the guard was satisfied nothing was amiss and resumed his rounds.

At once, Gino was up and ruthlessly divesting Rodolpho of his heavy sheepskin coat. He'd wrapped the child in it and made the stretch back to the shadows of the trees just as the guard returned to the front of the battlements. Dropping down in the shadows, he laid his hand firmly over the boy's mouth and whispered. "You must be very quiet, or they will kill us both. You know who I am, don't you?" The child's teat-filled eyes looked at him dumbly, and he nodded. "Then you know you can trust me to take care of you?" After a moment, the child nodded again, and Gino removed his hand with a smile.

"You're a brave little boy," he praised him softly, "and you're going to have to be braver for just a little while longer—but then everything will be all right, I promise! Do you believe me?"

"Yes," the boy choked, "but I'm *scared!*"

Gino stretched out his arms and cuddled the child awkwardly against him. "Shhh," he whispered. "Of course you're scared. I've been scared, too!"

"You have?" the boy's voice was incredulous.

"Of course. Everybody has times when they're scared," Gino said softly, "but it's always all right in the end, and it'll be all right this time, you'll see."

"But everybody's dead," the boy wailed despairingly. "Mamma, my sisters and brother, and now father. I'm all alone." He turned his head against Gino's chest with a wail, and wept uncontrollably, while Gino held him tightly and patted his mall shoulder consoling. "Shhhh. You're not entirely alone; you've got me."

For a long while, Gino sat in the tree shadows holding the boy in his arms, until suddenly the sobbing ceased and he realized the child was asleep. Then he wrapped it very carefully in Rodolpho's warm coat and laid the child on a bed of soft leaves. Now he would begin to carry out his own plans.

Standing up and stretching his weary body, Gino felt something slithering against his skin and unconsciously reached for it: the playing card! He stared at it almost superstitiously. So far the talisman had protected him—and the holy man in red had promised it would always protect him, always open every door.

But the only door it would need to open was in the castle, to get Francesca away from Prince Prospero. Gino had a plan—but suppose he lost his talisman? For safekeeping he tossed it down on the sleeping child. Then lightheartedly, he went about his task: gathering the strongest, longest, toughest wines in the underbrush.

Gino sat in the shadows beside the sleeping child and plaited his vines, testing them with his most vigorous yanks and jerks. Occasionally he discarded a length that seemed weak and likely to betray, but eventually he had a rope of sturdy greenery that was satisfactory. Now for something to serve as an anchor. Quietly he sought over the surrounding terrain, finding nothing but insubstantial dead wood branches. It would have to be a broken branch from a living tree. Again he surveyed the small woods, and found exactly what he needed.

It required two gigantic leaps before Gino caught the branch and exerted the weight of his body to wrench it from its tree, but finally it snapped and let Gino fall to earth, rolling painfully down a small rise. For a moment he lay breathless and still, suppressing a groan. Every part of his body ached wildly. After a while, he pulled himself together and scrambled to his feet. At least, he had the branch.

The child was still sleeping the sleep of exhaustion when Gino had completed his rough scaling ladder. Gino bent over the boy and tucked the sheepskin coat more securely about him. Then he stood up and debated: if the lad woke to find himself deserted?

Even if he screamed and ran out to his father's dead body, he'd be safe. Gino had heard Prospero's ringing command, "*Not the child!*" So no matter what sort of fuss the boy made at finding himself alone, he'd be safe from the archers—and perhaps Gino would return before he woke. After a further moment of internal debate, Gino leaned over and picked up the playing card. It was his talisman, after all, and now, if ever, was the moment he would need every aid he could get.

With a final glance at the sleeping child, Gino turned to the castle, holding the absurd rope of plaited vines with its anchor of a tree branch. Quietly and cautiously, he stole to the edge of the wood shadows again, and listened. Strangely, it seemed the guard must have been withdrawn from the battlements, for Gino heard no more footsteps, no clink of metal as the sword touched the parapet in the sentry's rounds.

For a long while he waited, mistrustful of the absence of sound. At last he told himself, *The man has gone below for his replacement, perhaps . . .* or it was conceivable he might be catching forty winks? Have to chance it, Gino decided, and stole forward to the highest rise of ground, judging his distance carefully in the moonlight. With a healthy heave, he tossed the tree branch upward and sighed with relief as it soared over the crenellated parapet, to catch between the masonry.

There was still no sound from above. Hugging the castle wall, Gino tested his rope of plaited vines, crawling up a few hand-holds and hauling viciously at the greenery.

It held.

With a long breath of determination, Gino cast the die: he went up his rope, hand over hand, as swiftly as possible until he neared the top. Now he was more cautious; as his foot scraped the stones, he froze briefly, but there was still no motion from the sentry, and Gino finally reached the top. He peered swiftly each way, but saw nothing. The coast seemed entirely clear; the guard must be around at the back of the castle roof. Rapidly, he pulled himself over the parapet, and turned to reel in his makeshift grappling hook and ladder.

Behind him there was the sound of clashing chain mail, the clatter of a sword, a falling body. Gino froze, then whirled, sensing someone right behind him. In his hands he raised the tree branch, as the only possible protection against a blow—and the only way to inflict one.

"Gently, my son," said the warm affectionate voice, and Gino slowly lowered the tree branch with a sigh that was near to a faint. Before him stood the monk in his red habit, the hood obscuring his face as always. "Remain here," he went on, "and shortly after the tolling of one, I will send Francesca to you."

"I must get to her now," Gino protested.

"You've recovered your courage," the man in red told him, "now prove your wisdom. There is nothing you can do now, there are too many. Wait, as I tell you."

"The guards will discover me," Gino countered, anxiously.

"No, you have nothing to fear," the voice was gently amused. "Look there . . ."

Obediently, Gino followed the gesture and went forward to a shadowy corner of the roof. Before him was the crumpled figure of a guard. Briefly, Gino hesitated, but the man did not move, and remembering the cup of wine brought to the battlements earlier, Gino thought perhaps there had been other cups of wine. With a wry twist of his lips, he wondered what Prince Prospero would say to a guard, drunk on duty?

Cautiously he went a few steps closer and dropped to one knee to peer at the man. One glance, and Gino recoiled in horror . . . for the guard's face was bedewed with blood, his arms flung out in the final embrace of the Red Death.

Gino turned swiftly and sprang to his feet—but the Man in Red had vanished . . .

Chapter XI

WITHIN HER TINY ROOM at the top of the castle, Esmeralda was dressing for the masque, with an occasional pat for the grayhound as she flitted about. Her costume was that of a butterfly, and Esmeralda was struggling to fasten the wings properly, when there was a tap at the door.

"Yes?" she said, turning hopefully. Perhaps it was one of the servants who would help her. "Come in."

The door swung open to admit Hop-Toad in all his fearsome African war paint, and involuntarily Esmeralda suppressed a scream, shrinking back against the miniscule dressing table.

"Forgive me for frightening you," the dwarf said contritely. "It's only Hop-Toad made more ugly than even he is, for the masque, you know."

"You are *never* ugly to me, the midget ballerina said quickly, recovering herself. "It was only—I hadn't known what your costume was to be, and you are—realistic!"

He laughed sardonically, and as Esmeralda looked at him inquiringly, he said, "Yes, I fancy I *am* realistic tonight, but that's unimportant. I came to say there's no need for you to appear at the masque."

"I don't understand," she stared at him, bewildered.

Hop-Toad came forward and took her hand warmly.

"My plans are made. If you will trust me and believe that I'll protect you, we'll leave this monstrous castle tonight."

"Do we dare? she murmured, staring at him with frightened eyes. "Outside there is the—Red Death."

"It can be no worse than life here," he said grimly, pressing her hand tightly. "Can you believe in me?"

"Oh yes," Esmeralda said instantly. "I do believe in you!"

"Then have a warm cloak and be ready," the dwarf smiled at

her, "for the game is almost over.

Closing Esmeralda's door, Hop-Toad scrambled swiftly down stairs to knock at the Duke of Malaga's bedchamber. "Shall we begin the performance, *Excellenzia*?"

In the ballroom below, the revellers had settled to enjoyment. A falcon danced with a rabbit; harlequin made amorous advances to a bar wench, while a tipsy leopard did a sensuous solo to its own crooning rhythm. As Hop-Toad had prophesied, despite the grandeur of the scene, the costumes *were* ordinary—and Alfredo's appearance at the head of the stairs did create sensation!

The Duke let out a grunting cry and lumbered down the stairs as the guest instinctively shrank away. A number of the ladies screamed pleasantly, and Hop-Toad appeared, swinging his tiny whip, loops of rope coiled over his shoulder.

"Have no fear!" he cried, burlesquing wildly. "This great beast has come from Africa. It is wild and dangerous, yet *I* can control this monster. Make way, there, if you please . . ."

Alfredo shambled toward the guests and threw himself into his performance gleefully. He crouched and grunted; he made small jumps and skips, with menacing gestures and snarls—and the ladies shrieked in fright that was not entirely assumed. The Duke was absolutely delighted with his effect, while Hop-Toad rapidly unfastened the chandelier chain, lowered it some distance and refastened it.

"Fear not!" the dwarf returned to his own performance, uncoiling his shoulder rope. "I will tie him up and make him helpless."

Now some of the guests began to laugh at the play, while Hop-Toad tied Alfredo securely, threw the end over the chandelier and fastened it. "What are you doing you fool?" Alfredo protested in an angry undertone, but Hop-Toad only muttered, "Listen! Our charade is well received; hear the laughter!" Running to the chandelier chain, he drew it up with powerful leaves of his strong arms, and fastened it so the Duke dangled far over the heads of the guests, who now laughed even more heartily.

Picking up a bottle of brandy, the dwarf nimbly scampered up the chandelier chair angling from the side wall, while the Duke in his ape's costume struggled wildly and bellowed, "Let me down, you ugly creature. You've gone too far. I'll beat you to death for this!"

Amid the gales of laughter, Prospero sat on his throne chair with Francesca beside him, and enjoyed Alfredo's discomfiture thoroughly. "Look, my dear," he said, laughing heartily. "I do believe our clever Hop-Toad is playing a joke on Alfredo!"

The Duke had abandoned all pretense of a game, and as the dwarf neared him along the chandelier chain, he roared, "Let me down at once, d'you here! I'll set you to tortures unimagined!"

"You have already tortured by your casual cruelty to my Esmeralda," Hop-Toad told him softly. "Now is the moment of reckoning."

"Let me down!"

Hop-Toad only looked down at the guests and called out, "The great African ape says it wants some brandy." Swiftly, he emptied his bottle over the furry costume, and with calm deliberation, reached for a candle from the chandelier—and set the Duke aflame. Alfredo let out one long scream, and the laughter from the crowd stopped in a breathless concerted gasp of horror, as the dwarf slid down the chandelier chain, eluded a guard, and raced away.

The rope burned away and Alfredo fell heavily, a flaming mass in the center of the ballroom floor, as the guest hastily got out of the way. Francesca was by now so dulled with exhaustion and the horror of the past days, that she merely sat, impassive.

"I see you no longer turn away from the cruelties of life?" Prospero observed.

"I no longer care," she agreed. "My life is done. What's left I give to you tonight."

The Prince turned toward her eagerly, with a triumphant smile. Evidently, he thought he'd won in his campaign to corrupt her, but as she stared at him expressionlessly, she felt a flash of inner sardonic amusement. It was not going to turn out as he expected, not at all! She meant to keep the promise she'd made to Juliana: When the time comes, I shall not lose my courage.

So tonight, even as Prospero embraced her, she would kill him . . . and herself. "But at least have *that* taken away," she requested calmly, and with a gesture, Prospero summoned a guard.

"Clear that out of the way. How can my guests dance? And when Hop-Toad is found, give him six pieces of gold for his entertaining jest." With a salute, the guard went away, summoning a couple of servants to aid his grisly task, while Prospero turned back to Francesca. "You've pleased me very much, Francesca," he began softly . . . and suddenly leaned forward with a strangled gasp, gripping her wrists convulsively.

"What is it?" she asked, startled, and involuntarily swivelled to follow his gaze.

"There again," Prospero muttered. A man dressed in a scarlet hooded cloak."

"I see no one," she said, bewildered.

With a sigh, he released her wrists and sat back, speaking half to himself. "Perhaps not. I forbade anyone to masquerade in such a costume . . ." Grimly, his eyes peered about in the throng before him, while Francesca gently massaged her wrists, and at last, he abandoned his search and turned to her again. "Ah, forgive me!" he apologized tenderly, and raised her aching wrists to his lips, one after the other, looking into her eyes with a meaning smile . . . only to release her sharply with another grunt of displeasure.

"There, beyond the windows," he said, springing up in great agitation. "I'm positive I saw a red costume. Wait here for me."

Swiftly, the Prince went down the steps from the dais and thrust his way though the dancers, stretching to his full height in order to look over their heads. Let alone in her chair, Francesca watched him in surprise. For whom did he seek? Unconsciously her own eyes moved about, and for a brief moment as the swirling skirts of a street dancer costume fell into place about feminine legs, Francesca did think she saw a flash of ruby red beyond—but it was instantly lost to view. Perhaps it was only a trick of the candlelight that struck such brilliant sparks from the jewels of embroidery and necklace . . .

Sinking back into her chair again, Francesca composed herself to waiting. She had not the least notion as to why a *red* costume should be so distressing to Prince Prospero, but she had long since abandoned any attempt at the mental agility needed to understand his whims. Instead, she concentrated on the inner courage she would need when he returned. In a way, it was an added torment to be forced to delay, for with every added moment of suspense before the crisis of her destiny, Francesca knew herself growing wearier, both physically and mentally.

"Pray God, I'm not too *tired* to kill him when the time comes!" she told herself sardonically.

Meanwhile, Prince Prospero made his way across the ballroom to the long French windows leading onto the terrace—but there was no Man in Red visible among the amorous couples who'd sought its darkness. Standing against the window, Prospero's eyes darted keenly about the revellers and rose over their heads—and again, it seemed a figure stood at the entrance to the Yellow Room, in a flash of red.

Wildly, Prospero pushed the dancers from his path and strode to that door, but there were only a few couples here, and two lovers on the small golden couch. "Did a figure in a scarlet cloak pass through here?" he cried, but they shook their heads.

"We saw no one, Prospero," they told him, continuing their dance. "Leave the door open, or we cannot hear the music!"

The Prince ran past them to the Purple Room, that was also filled with revellers, drinking and stuffing themselves with dainties from the plates on the side table—and now he *distinctly* saw the hem of a red robe just disappearing into the White Room. Tight-lipped with anger, he strode past the guests and through to the black door, while behind him, the guests continued their dancing. Throwing open the final door, Prospero entered in a fury.

"Who are you that dares to disregard my commands?" he demanded. "I said that no one—*no one*—was to masquerade as the Red Death! How dare you disobey me!"

The Man in Red stood calmly by the altar. "I am not in costume, Prince Prospero," he said, in his soft, affectionate voice.

Slowly, Prospero moved forward, peering through the darkness but unable to see the face within the great hood. "I cannot see through the shadows," he whispered. "All is black."

"There is no face of Death until the moment of your own Death—and I am only one of many messengers."

"Who do you come for?" Prospero asked, faintly frightened yet still confident of his own immunity.

"Many."

"All?" Prospero held his breath.

"Not quite all," said the Man in Red.

"Aha, I knew I was right," Prospero exulted with a great laugh of relief. "I have won!"

Whirring faintly, the great clock tolled once and was silent. One o'clock, and time to unmask!

In the outer rooms, there were sounds of happy laughter, incredulity, joyous surprise, as the guests removed their masks and recognized each other in a babble of amusement.

The Man in Red shifted his gaze from Prospero toward the confusion beyond. "The hour of unmasking," he observed. "Now they show their naked faces." Slowly he moved forward past the Prince, who turn and followed at his side, like a host about to introduce a new and valued guest. "It's time for a new dance to begin," the Man in Red continued, stepping into the White Room and touching the two remaining dancers lightly. "The Dance of Death."

Before Prospero's eyes, the gorgeous costumes of satin and velvet seemed changed to gauze and cheapest sateen. The faces of the dancers, too, were suddenly exposed. Beneath the harsh white light of reality, the beautiful complexions of paint and powder disappeared, leaving feverish cheeks, pale lips, ghastly gray-white skin seemingly stretched to tightly over their skulls. Fascinated, Prospero paused to study the lacklustre eyes that seemed sunken . . . the change in the dance rhythm: no more the graceful posturing of court dance, but an awkward jerky quickened pace that resembled nothing so much as mechanical dolls.

"Fantastic!" he murmured to himself in sudden excitement, and found himself left behind, as the Man in Red passed leisurely along into the Purple Room. Prospero hastened after him, to observe the same gentle touch on the dancers—and the same alteration to the mad dance of death.

"Our Master will be pleased!" Prospero said proudly. "I brought all these souls to him. I taught them his worship, and corrupted them for him."

The Man in Red made no reply but went on to the throng in the Yellow Room, and set them dancing at a touch—but in his gestures was only gentleness and a strange fatherly sadness. Almost, he sighed, as he passed along to the main ballroom.

At his side, Prince Prospero strode along happily. "I knew he was supreme when no one else did," he stated ingratiatingly. "I built a chapel to Satan and prayed to him, and made a pact with him."

Now the Man in Red silently entered the great hall, where the unmasked guests were dancing gaily, the excitement of recognition past. Signora Escobar was reunited with Signor Veronese; Lampredi and Clistor held hands languidly and waltzed together. Anna-Marie had already found another protector to replace the Duke of Malaga, and was solidifying her position with coy simperings, interspersed with occasional tiny peeks at the charms she had to offer.

With growing pride, the Prince watched his new guest pass through the room. A touch here, a touch there, a faint gesture, a snap of the fingers—and everyone was doing the new dance! At last he stood beside the Man in Red, their backs to the great hall clock, looking out over the room. Only Francesca still sat in her chair, gazing at the Man in Red with wonder, but without fear, while Prospero was almost smirking with pride of achievement.

"I promised them safety," he confided with a chuckle.

"You presumed too much," the Man in Red remarked, and the Prince hastened to make amends.

"I know, I know . . . but in a way it makes a fine jest, does it not? The kind of jest that amuses Satan . . ."

"Does it?" The soft voice beside him was noncommittal and Prospero suppressed a frown. This strange messenger had no sense of humor? Incredible!

His eye caught the figure of Francesca—waiting. "Your excellency," he said quickly, "that girl—spare her."

"A charitable request," the Man in Red commented idly, "or is it that you have—other plans for her? Charity is a rare thing with you, Prospero." His Highness chuckled involuntarily; the messenger did, after all, have understanding! Almost he extended an elbow to dig the man in the ribs!

Looking directly at Francesca, the Man in Red said to her with a soft affectionate clarity that cut across the growing chaos among the dancers, "Go to the battlements, my daughter. *Go now!*"

In response to that warm voice, Francesca stood up. Then she hesitated, glancing at Prospero. "Go on, my dear," he said. "I'll meet you when this is all over."

Swiftly, almost joyously, Francesca obeyed. Oh, to be rid of this sickening display, to feel the cold clear air of heaven against her face once more, to breathe freedom for the last time! Without a glance at the frenetic dancers on the ballroom floor, she slipped down the steps from the dais and skirted the throng, making for the doorway and the staircase leading upward. She was conscious of a faint bewilderment: the Prince had been so disturbed by the thought of a guest wearing a *red* costume—yet now he stood beside just such a guest, and his pose was almost one of exultation.

Still, it was the Man in Red who had given her these last moments of freedom and air. As Francesca half-ran toward the stairs, she was mindful of her manners. "Thank you, thank you!" she murmured, and would have reached to kiss the hand that granted her respite.

Yet even as she curtseyed before him and extended her fingers, he drew back sharply. "I give you a sign," the warm voice whispered, and before her eyes, thin white fingers flicked an oblong decorated with an unfamiliar design. Wonderingly, Francesca took the card. "Rise, my daughter," said the voice, "and make haste on your way to the battlements. Stop for nothing and no one, do you hear?"

"Yes," Francesca bowed her head obediently and rose from her curtsey. Holding the card in both hands, she ran up the stairs, still under the spell of command.

As she disappeared into the upper hall, turning toward the second flight of stairs, Prospero said, almost as an afterthought, "Thank you, your Excellency."

The Man in Red turned, tilting his head to look at the Prince quizzically, and Prospero added in explanation. "For the girl . . ."

"I have no title," the monk remarked. "Why do you call me 'excellency'?"

"I thought, as an ambassador from Satan . . ."

"He is not *my* master. Death has no master."

"Still, Satan rules the universe," Prospero said cheerfully, "and I have made a pact with him."

"He does not rule alone, and your pact with him will not save you," the Man in Red said softly.

Prospero turned to stare at his unusual guest, suddenly alarmed.

"But there is no other God; Satan killed him," he protested, half-screaming.

"That is your mistake." The voice was bleak. "There are as many Gods as human hearts—and many heavens, and as many hells as those hearts make for themselves." Before Prospero's starting eyes, the thin bony fingers threw back the shadowing hood of the red monk's habit and the Prince recoiled sharply . . . *for the face of the Red Death was a mirror image of his own, bedewed with blood drops.*

"Your hell, Prince Prospero, and the moment of your death," the velvety voice murmured, as Prospero shrank away in terror and turned in flight.

"No! *Nooooooo!*" The Prince screamed involuntarily, and desperately rushed away into the maelstrom of death-dancers jigging wildly about the ballroom.

"*Yeeeessss,*" the dancers sighed inexorably, moving past him with outstretched hands. "Join us, join us, Prospero . . ."

Balling his fists the Prince smashed a path through them to the long French windows—only to pull up short, his mouth falling open in a silent scream.

The Man in Red faced him, smiling softly. One long hand reached toward Prospero, who feinted sideways and raced away from that touch of death. Back he ran through the dancers—and now there were some who seemingly exhausted by the pace of the dance, had fallen to the floor, not to rise again. As Prospero cut his path across the ballroom, he swerved time and again, or leaped over the fallen—yet could not fail to notice their bloodied faces.

In total panic, Prospero muttered to himself grimly, *"I* shall win, it is all a mistake. I must reach the Black Room and there I shall be safe." It seemed he was not destined for his sanctuary, for whichever way he turned among the dancers—who were now dropping like flies—every exit was blocked by the figure of the Man in Red. Again and again, Prospero pulled up in the nick of time, just before that fatal touch could reach him.

He was beginning to be faint with the exertion of trying to divert the Man in Red long enough to gain the entrance to the series of rooms lading to the Black Door, but at long last he made it. Glancing over his shoulder as he darted into the Yellow Room, he could see the mean in Red moving swiftly but nevertheless still behind him— so there was yet hope for Prospero. Racing through the succession of rooms, the Prince was aware of the blood-spattered faces of his guests, lying immobile, grotesque, clutching and rigid in death.

With a sob of fright, Prince Prospero recoiled from the evidences of disaster and glanced over his shoulder hauntedly—to meet the placid smile of the Man in Red, following unhurriedly. Turning back, the Prince plunged onward into the Black Room, slamming and bolting the door behind him and hastening forward to cast himself before the altar with its flickering inner flames. "Satan, my master," he mumbled wildly, "save me, protect me, for I am your most faithful servant and will have no other master but you."

Beyond the altar there was a rustle of motion, and Prospero raised his eyes hopefully.

The Man in Red moved from the corner shadows as smoothly, as suavely, as ever Prospero had moved to order an execution, and in the blood-red light of the window in the wall over the altar, his face was that of the Prince himself.

"Why will you fight me?" the voice said in soft regret. "It is useless!" The long arm reached forward definitively, as Prospero shrank away, half-mad with fear and hysteria, but there was no hiding place. As the fingers tapped his shoulder gently, he screamed in agony and tumbled backward to the floor. The Man in Red bent toward him sadly. "You of all men should welcome me. After all, your soul has been dead for a long time."

Throwing his hands to his face, Prospero felt dewy droplets springing forth. Trembling, he extended his fingers and identified the liquid.

It was blood—thick and viscous.

Prospero threw out his arms and screamed again, once . . .

The Man in Red straightened up and surveyed him with mingled pity and contempt. "So much for your bargains with Satan," he murmured with a sigh, and made his way leisurely from the room.

Slowly, critically, he passed through the White Room, the Purple Room, the Yellow Room, and back to the main ballroom. Here a scant dozen guest still danced although there was no music from the orchestra gallery where the men slumped over their instru-ments. Swiftly, the Man in Red moved forward to the remaining dancers and tapped them imperiously on the shoulders. Then he passed on to the entrance doors of the castle, and stood a moment in contemplation while one after another of the dancers fell to the floor and lay still.

When there was no more movement anywhere, the Man in Red took a deep breath and swivelled about the room as he exhaled gen-tly—and all the candles in the brilliant wall sconces flickered and went out. Last of all, he looked up at the great crystal chandelier and spared it a separate *whuff!* that smothered its light instantly.

Now there was only the moonlight, striking through the long french windows. The Man in Red took a final glance, and turned out to the flagged courtyard, walking across to the gatehouse at the drawbridge. "Luigi," he called, softly commanding, and within the guard's quarters, a voice said sleepily, "Who calls?"

"It is I, the master. Come forth and lower the bridge."

Rapidly, there was the sound of flint, a lighted candle, and Luigi emerged, tucking his trousers awkwardly. *"Yes,* your Highness." He applied himself to the ropes and chains with a will, and the bridge fell with a crash as the portcullis rose with a clatter. Only then did Luigi turn toward the figure waiting in the courtyard and widened his eyes.

"Who are you?" he demanded, suddenly wide awake and laying a hand to his sword. "You're not Prince Prospero."

"No," the Man in Red admitted softly. "I am greater than he."

"There's no one greater," Luigi said flatly, and sprang back to the winches. "You had me fooled, that you did! Never did I hear a voice more like his, but you won't get *me* into trouble. His High-ness said 'seal the castle', and scaled she'll stay until he gives me the proper word."

But Luigi had time for no more than a single turn to lower the gate, when the Man in Red stood beside him, his hand extended in a light touch. With a gurgle, the gateman sank down over his cables and chains, while the monk pursed his lips thoughtfully and evaluated the state of the portcullis: was it secure enough, or might it crash downward when least expected?

At last the Man in Red thrust aside Luigi's dead weight and gave a twist to the winch, raising the portcullis to its full extent and securing it with a competent hitch of the ropes. Then with leisurely dignity he went across the bridge and stood on the far side of the moat, on the road leading to Estaban.

"*Holá*, you above—Gino, Francesca!" he called lazily, yet the voice cut clearly through the night air, and in the shadows of the battlements there was a cautious movement. The Man in Red laughed softly. "Come forth, there is no need for fear," he said, and saw Gino's face, a small white blur in the darkness, peering down from the parapet.

"Listen carefully and obey me! Come you down through the castle to the main courtyard, where you will find the gate open and the bridge in place," he said, "but *touch nothing and no one* in your passage, you understand?"

"*Yes!*" Francesca's voice rang out clearly, confidently, even as Gino hesitated. "We will do as you say—but where shall we go?"

"To Estaban," the Man in Red called, almost surprised. "You will rebuild, for now all is purged and cleansed. Have no fear, and accept those who come to aid you."

Again it was Francesca's clear voice that answered. "We will— but will you not wait for us? Can we not aid you?"

In the moonlight, the lips beneath the great shadowing red hood curved in a tender smile. "No, there is naught you can do for me, save to obey my commands. I bid you farewell . . . farewell!"

Leaning over the battlements with Gino's arms protectively about her, Francesca watched the tall figure striding away over the hill toward Estaban. "I could wish he had stayed," she murmured. "Little as we will have, I *know* we could have found something with which to make him welcome in thanks for his help."

"Already on the hillside I had told him he would ever be wel- come in our home," Gino reminded her, "when he gave me the card."

Francesca looked down at the card in her own hands. "He said it was a sign," she remembered, extending it and peering at it closely in the moonlight, "but I do not know what it means. Do you, Gino?"

He drew out his own card and held it beside hers. Once more the soft rose-red of the ace of hearts glowed gently in his hands.

Looking at the austere figure portrayed on Francesca's card, he said suddenly, "I am quite certain these are called Hearts. Mine is the higher in value, I think—but yours is one of the Court cards: the Queen." Staring at the cards, he laughed suddenly and hugged her. "A sign indeed!" he said. "See—they are decorated with hearts! What better for you and me, my darling? And even if my card is worth more than yours, well—are you not the queen of my heart, and am I not supreme in yours, hmmmm?"

Snuggled against him, Francesca could feel lighthearted once more. "Of course that is what they mean," she agreed happily, and reaching up to kiss his cheek fleetingly. For a moment they clung together, until she shivered involuntarily in the cold night air, and Gino said at once, "We must go; you are cold . . ."

She shivered again, with fright. "Do we dare believe him?" she whispered.

"I think we have to trust in him," Gino said after a moment. "He is a holy man, that much is certain from his garb . . . and actually, he has spoken truth both to Concetta and to me, and to you! We failed to understand his words, but they have been the truth.

"The day of our deliverance from Prospero *was* at hand," Gino said somberly, even if it came through our deaths rather than his."

"Yes, that is so," Francesca agreed. "Very well, let us try to reach the opened bridge—but I will go first, Gino. "No," as he started to protest, "if there is any difficulty below, *I* will be the one who can surmount it, not you. Stay in the shadows behind me, until we are certain all is safe, and vanish *instantly* should anyone intercept me."

"But . . . I know I am right," she interrupted firmly, "What is to be gained if you should be killed in trying to protect me when I feel certain I am quite safe from harm?" Her lips twisted drily. "I assure you, Prospero won't permit anyone or anything to harm me—yet! Not until he is positive he can never get what he wants . . . and at the moment, he thinks he is in sight of his goal. No, hang back, Gino, and wait; then you will give *me* strength. No matter what happens, I shall know you're alive—when I'd thought you dead," she caught her breath in a sob of remembering anguish, "but so long as you're alive, somewhere, I can keep my courage to face anything. You must promise me!"

"All right," he said reluctantly. "I suppose you're right. Indeed the monk told me much the same thing earlier here on these battlements—but it is hard to hold my hand when you are concerned, Francesca!"

"Nevertheless," she said firmly, "he stayed you before—and was he not right? You would only have died at the hands of the mob below—and eventually, I came to you at his command. Oh, Gino—let us obey him carefully!"

"Yes, very well," Gino agreed, leaning over the parapet cautiously. "The bridge *is* down and the gate drawn up. Perhaps we should make a run for it. Lead the way then, and if we are caught, I promise to hide until you give the signal. It strikes me," he murmured drily, "that you are becoming uncommon shrewd in dealing with difficulties!"

"Not really," she assured him anxiously, twisting around to look at him in the moonlight. "It's only that I've realized there are things I can do and say because I'm a woman, where you would instantly be flogged for the same things. I never knew that before, Gino."

He caught her against him in a bear-hug. "I know you didn't, my dearest one," he murmured with an involuntary chuckle. "I love you, do you know that?" With a long breath he pressed his lips to hers. "All right," he said finally, letting her go with a sigh. "Lead the way."

Softly, Francesca stole down the staircase from the battlements, reconnoitering at each curve and beckoning for Gino to follow. There were still the flaming wall torches lighting the landings and the corridors, but as she crept downward, she was aware of death-like silence below.

What had become of the orchestra music, the footsteps of the dancers, the laughter of the guests? If the party were over, where was Prince Prospero?

Trembling, she stood at the head of the great staircase and saw only blackness below. Apparently all the candles had been extinguished, yet the clock still ticked majestically. To her ears, it was a comforting sound; something lived . . .

Gino stole down to put his arms about her. "What's wrong? he whispered in her ear.

"I don't know," she breathed almost soundlessly, "but—I don't understand the darkness and silence below." Hesitantly, she turned and went along the corridor to her chamber, pushing open the door softly. Within all seemed normal, with a small fire sparkling in the grate and candles gleaming softly on dressing table and night stands.

Francesca walked forward with sudden confidence—for beneath the candle-glimmer from the bedside table, she had caught a reassuring sight: across the bed lay a thick cloak, and upon it gleamed her own polished wood cross!

The Man in Red had said: "Touch nothing and no one . . ." Francesca stayed her involuntary outthrust of hand and debated briefly. He could *never* have meant she should abandon her cross? Surely, no matter what disasters might have overcome the castle, no matter what horror might still face her, her cross and all it touched would be immune and a protection forever!

With sudden decision, Francesca reached forward and picked up her cross. Then she picked up the heavy cloak on which it had lain and threw it about her, snuggling gratefully into its warmth and concealment. There was no doubt it would be bitter cold beyond the bridge, even if she and Gino could achieve it in safety. Swiftly she whirled and ran back to the door, reconnoitering briefly, but there was still only silence. Gino came forward anxiously from the shadows beyond the staircase, and she laid a finger on her lips.

"I still go first," she whispered in his ear compellingly. "Stay here; if the way is clear, I'll hoot like a night owl—and if anyone accosts me, you promised not to interfere! You will go back to the battlements, or take refuge in my room beneath the bed—you saw which door?"

Gino nodded reluctantly. "I don't like this," he muttered. "Let me come with you."

"No," she hissed, and started quietly down the stairs. Her heart pounded with terror at each step, expecting—she knew not what, but in this household it could only be additional horror. Two things sustained her: the steady ticking of the great clock, and the feel of the playing card the Man in Red had given her as a symbol. Francesca had tucked it into the pocket of the cloak together with her beloved cross, and now her fingers closed convulsively over her talismans.

"Lord, protect me!" she prayed silently, and stepped down onto the marble floor of the hall.

Behind her the clock continued to tick rhythmically, as Francesca bent forward to peer cautiously between the draperies of the ballroom entrance. It was bathed in brilliant moonlight, and apparently carpeted with motionless figures. Francesca stood still and stared. She could see no slightest sign of life anywhere throughout the room, and even as she gave the hoot-owl signal for Gino to join her, she frowned in bewilderment. Had the guests really drunk so much as to pass out in that way?

Gino was beside her now, and she abandoned consideration of the ways of the aristocracy in favor of opening the great double doors. Below were the magnificent entrance stairs curving down to the courtyard, but all was bathed in clearest moonlight.

Momentarily, Gino and Francesca clung to each other in the shadows of the doorway. Suppose there were an archer with his bow trained for any movement across the path to the bridge? "He will never shoot a woman's figure," Francesca said flatly. "So you will sidle around the edges in the darkness while I walk straight across. Yes! I know that is what we should do—and I shall walk very slowly and deliberately. If anyone is watching he will be watching *me;* nobody will notice your movement at the side. Come on!"

Steadily, she walked down the main steps from the castle entrance. Deliberately, indolently, languidly, she drifted across the flags, her head held high, her chin raised defiantly to the moon. *Let them kill me,* she thought; *Gino will get away.* She was aware of minute motions around to the side, and her heart surged with hope. Nearly to the bridge, and as the Man in Red had promised, it was open—but now she saw a motionless shape slumped beside the winches! With a throb of fright, she hastened ahead, as Gino bent over—then recoiled! He slid around the figure to intercept her. "Don't look!" he commanded softly. "He's dead . . . of the Red Death!"

Francesca buried her face in his shoulder and shuddered. "We must go! It is only to get across the bridge—and we will be free . . ."

"Shhh, yes, he murmured, but even as they turned for the final steps, Francesca's ears discerned motion somewhere in the darkness behind them and she shrank back.

"Drop down!" she hissed vehemently, and obediently he crouched in the shadow, while Francesca stepped into full moonlight and defiantly waited for the rustlings to assume definite form. For a long moment she stood motionless. Then a voice whispered hoarsely, "Milady, it is I, Hop-Toad."

Francesca nearly fainted with inward relief. "What do you here?" she whispered back.

"I would save myself and Esmeralda, with your aid, milady."

Accept those who come to aid you, the Man in Red had told them . . .

"The Bridge is down, the keeper is dead of the Red Death," she muttered from the corner of her mouth, "but we know not what surveillance may remain."

"But milady," Hop-Toad inserted softly, "the castle is dead. Did you not know?" She whirled on him as he emerged from the shadows with the tiny dancer beside him. "There is no life in it, but the four of us," he said quietly, "and so—no need to fear."

"Prospero?" she whispered anxiously.

"Dead of the Red Death, together with his guests in the ballroom," the dwarf said simply, and as Gino came from his hiding place, "Good evening to you, sir. Shall we go forth together?"

With a courtly grace, Hop-Toad handed Esmeralda's tiny figure across the drawbridge to the outer road. "Milady?" Gino extended his hand in awkward imitation of the dwarf, and they followed the tiny couple across to the road, where all four of them breathed deep and looked at each other with tentative smiles.

"Wither?" Francesca said, looking at Gino.

Before he could answer, there was a frightened wail from the tree shadows. "The child!" Gino ran forward hastily. "I had nearly forgot. Hush," he cried, "I am coming."

Francesca picked up her skirts and raced after him, while the dancer and the dwarf looked at each other hesitantly. "Let us stay with them," she murmured pleadingly. "I feel—oh, it's not that I don't have faith in you, Ernesto! But in this world . . . they are full-sized, and they are kindly. Please let us go with them."

"Of course, if you wish it," he said, steadying her along the rutted road, "And I think that you are wise, my love. I would lay down my life for you gladly—but that would not be very helpful, would it?" He chuckled. "No, until we are settled, such as we must needs have protectors—and these will be kind to us."

Beneath the trees, they found Francesca cuddling the little boy in her arms. "You see, it is all right after all, Pietro," she crooned, rocking him back and forth. "Ah, it has been a hard time for you, I know, but now you are safe. You will stay with Gino and me, and we will build a lovely new house for all of us, shhhh."

"Yes, but," said Gino, troubled, "there is no lovely new house for this night, Francesca. Where shall we go? How shall we keep you warm, you and Pietro and the little lady?"

There was a momentary dismal silence, and the dwarf snapped his fingers, excitedly. "I have it!" he said. "There is a small cabin on the far side of the castle, formerly used by Prospero's shepherds, but abandoned when he turn the flocks over to the nearby village. I'll wager it's still there and not in to bad repair."

"Lead the way, Gino said instantly, and the little company set forth behind Hop Toad, who went forward slowly, moving this way and that through the trees until he found the half-hidden path that led down behind the castle. With a grunt of satisfaction, be beckoned and they felt their way after him. Francesca carried the child, Pietro, who was once more asleep, and Gino stretched a sturdy arm down for Esmeralda's tiny hand to grasp, but despite her best efforts, the midget ballerina was shortly gasping for breath and stumbling with weariness.

"By your leave, milady," said Gino, and swung her up into his arms to be carried like a child. "If your man can lead us, I'll not let his lady be overtired," he told her with a smile, and strode after Francesca and Hop-Toad, as Esmeralda nestled into his arms with an answering smile.

"Here we are!" the dwarf cried proudly, loosing the hasp on the rude shepherd's cottage and throwing back the door. "Esmeralda?" he turned back anxiously.

"Here I am, Ernesto," she said softly. "Gino was so kind as to carry me."

Carefully, Gino set the midget on her feet and smiled at Hop-

Toad's solicitude. "Now, we must have a fire," he said briskly. "I see a lantern and tinder; do you bring it, Ernesto, and let us see if they have left us any firewood."

The survivors of Prince Prospero's masque sat before a comfortable fire and made happy plans, while Pietro slept peaceful in his wrapping of Rodolpho's sheepskin coat, a small hand lying trustfully in Francesca's.

We would wish to join with you," Hop-Toad said with dignity, "if you will permit? I am stronger than I look—but more important: I know every part of Prince Prospero's terrain, and where food may be found."

"Of course you will join with us," Francesca said warmly, leaning over to pat Esmeralda's hand, while Gino and Hop-Toad discussed practical ways and means. Shortly, everyone was talking eagerly, even laughing merrily when Esmeralda observed. "I've never learned to cook because I couldn't reach the baking ovens." She chuckled at their amusement. "All the same, I have my uses," she said soberly. "I am a famous seamstress; *that* will be helpful." She looked at the dwarf with a faint sigh. "For the rest, I fear my talents will do little for your comfort, Ernesto: growing glowers, giving a sparkle to fine crystal or silver." She shrugged wryly. "Not what will be needed now."

"On the contrary, my love," Hop-Toad said firmly. "Exactly what's needed: someone to give a sparkle to our lives!"

"Bravo," Gino smiled at him, while Francesca was already promising to teach Esmeralda how to cook, "and we will build your ovens *low!*"

"There is the matter of money," the dwarf said to Gino, 'and here, too I can be useful." In response to Gino's look of inquiry, he said, "Our ladies are bejewelled by Prince Prospero. I venture to say they will have no wish to retain these—keepsakes!" His ugly face twisted sardonically. Yet, what more just solution than to covert his gems to ducats that will rebuild what *he* destroyed?" Gino nodded thoughtfully, and Hop-Toad finished, "In time, do you give me the baubles and I'll away to Florence, where *I* will know with whom to deal."

"Yes, " Gino agreed. "I confess I'd not know about such things.

I am only a peasant, after all."

"No longer," he said softly. "Now you are a landholder and the leader of a village we are going to build, that will owe allegiance only to itself!"

Somewhere a cock crowed triumphantly, and Francesca looked at Gino, bewildered. "Is it really dawn? I had thought it not far past two of the clock." She shivered in memory. "Oh, that dreadful great clock in the castle hall!"

Gino rose and peered from the door briefly. "The sun is rising," he said, with a smile. "The nightmare is over!" Kneeling down beside her, he held her close. "All will be well from now on and forevermore, he murmured.

Beyond the rude cottage there was only silence and moonlit peace, illuminating the hill at the outskirts of Estaban where the great tree still threw its stark shape against the sky. Somehow it was no longer threatening, in the faint presage of the new day.

Beneath the tree sat the Man in Red, laying out the Tarot cards idly. He looked up at the sound of an approaching footstep and raised a hand in greeting to a man cloaked in a black monk's habit. "Good morning, brother. Have you come far?"

"From Cathay and beyond. A hundred thousand perished at my passing this last night," the other said, looking out over the quiet countryside. "A pleasant spot, this one. I have not been here before."

"No," said the Man in Red, casually, "nor will you need to visit it soon again. It has been purged and made ready for rebuilding."

"Ah? Good!" said the Man in Black, as two more figures approached from the other side of the hill. One was dressed in saffron yellow, the other in white monk's habit. "The Man In Yellow sat down wearily. "This eternity of wandering! Ten thousand sleep where I walked. I am very tired."

"The weariness of those to whom we bring rest burdens you," the Man in White observed sympathetically. "And what of you, brother?" He turned to the Man in Red.

"I called many, he shrugged, gathering the Tarot cards together casually and rising to his feet. "Peasant and Prince, the worthy and the dishonored. Only five are left, a young man and woman, a dwarf and a tiny dancer, a small child. *Sic transit gloria mundi,"* he said with a sigh. "Shall we go?"

Together, the four monks walked across the hilltop, just as the first fingers of dawn burst up over the horizon. In the clear light, their habits glowed like jewels. At the edge of the clearing, the Man in Red paused to glance at Estaban. *"Requiescat in pace,"* he murmured sadly, as the others went past him. Briefly, he turned toward the wooded hills that intervened before the shepherd's cottage and raised his hand in a gesture of blessing. *"Vivat in pace,"* and his voice was once more warm with the tenderest affection.

Then the Man in Red turned away and in a few long strides had caught up to his brothers, taking his position between the Man in White and the Man in Yellow. Unhurriedly, the four moved on together . . .

THE END

Production Notes

Vincent Price and director Roger Corman, the masters of screen terror, have once again joined forces to make their seventh film together, and their first in England, "The Masque of The Red Death." Based on one of Edgar Allan Poe's most macabre and bizarre stories, it adds new dimensions to motion picture shock, terror and horror. An American International Pictures production, it is set in 12th century Italy, where Prince Prospero (Price), a devout worshiper of Satan, rules tyrannically in a land stricken by a mysterious plague. Prospero's cruel whims include toying with the fear-stricken peasants under his domain, in order to satisfy his own diabolical pleasures.

Also starring in the film is lovely Hazel Court, who appears for the third time in the successful Edgar Allan Poe series, after co-starring previously with Ray Milland in "The Premature Burial" and Vincent Price and Boris Karloff in "The Raven". For "The Masque of The Red Death" Court portrays Juliana, Prospero's beautiful companion in the pursuit of evil.

Jane Asher, a 17 year old redhead who made her first film at age 5, co-stars as Francesca, a young innocent who falls into Prospero's power when Gino, the man she loves is taken prisoner by the Prince.

David Weston, who recently played a featured role in "Becket," opposite Richard Burton, is the young hero Gino, who must rescue his beloved Francesca from the corrupt and wicked ways of Prospero's court.

Irish born stage actor Patrick Magee plays Alfredo, the Duke of Malaga, a sadist of strange and unique dimensions and another occupant of the castle retreat where an orgiastic masked Ball is held. Magee worked with director Roger Corman previously in "The Young Racers, as well as AIP's "Dementia 13."

Nigel Green rounds out the supporting cast in the role of Ludvico, Francesca's peasant father, who Prince Prospero brings to the castle for his own sadistic amusement. Green starred as Hercules in last years "Jason and the Argonauts" and was recently seen in "Zulu."

American International Pictures "The Masque of The Red Death" is the seventh and newest Poe thriller, filmed in vivid Pathecolor and wide-screen Panavision. It features a series of lavish and beautiful settings, designed to create a mood of terror.

Among the more luxurious sets are the 12th Century Palace, where the decadent Prince Prospero gathers the country's leading nobles behind his walls for a spectacular Ball, while the Red Death ravages the surrounding countryside.

The floors of Prince Prospero's central hall, which is featured in the film as both the main banqueting room and the setting for the masked Ball, are painted and varnished to represent Italian mala chite marble. The castle walls are made of simulated stone of the period, and are draped by five hundred yards of patterned silks. 350 flickering wax candles, especially designed in colors of blue, green, red and black cast their long spurting tongues of light on the scenes of debauchery, encouraged as entertainment by Prince Prospero.

"Thank you for coming to my orgy," joked Vincent Price as he passed amongst his guests after filming had ending on the wild and startling party sequences. Still in costume for his role of the depraved Prince Prospero, Price was thanking the crowds of extras who had played dissolute revelers during the film's climatic masked Ball. "At my age," gagged Price, "this is the only way you're likely to get to an orgy. All these years I've been looking for one in Hollywood, and haven't run across one yet. I did get an invitation, recently, to attend an orgy in Rome, but I guess it just came too late in life. Frankly I was nervous at the very idea. Screen orgies are the thing for me. This way, you can read the script and see exactly what's expected of you when you get there."

"Masque of the Red Death" is Price's sixth Poe film, and he has now become closely identified with this particular type of role. He regards this as a great compliment and views each new horrific assignment with great relish. "Working as we do from the stories of Edgar Allan Poe," explains Price, "we are able to film the peak of all that is great in horror fiction. But I prefer the term 'stories of terror' rather than 'horror' which makes most people think of monsters. For me, personally, however, kitchen sink dramas hold the greatest horrors. There's something unspeakably horrific about unwashed characters in sordid circumstances revealing aspects of their squalid lives. I'd run a mile from those dramas of so-called reality."

Director Roger Corman, 37, has made all six of AIP's previous Poe movies - including "House of Usher," "The Pit and The Pendulum," "Tales of Terror" and "The Raven." In "Masque of the Red Death" Corman has directed some of the most visually exciting scenes yet to be seen in the Poe series, one of the high spots being the masked Ball at which Death is an uninvited guest. For close-up shots where Prospero comes face to face with himself, immediately before meeting his own death, Corman insisted on a degree of realism by the use of real blood - donated by a local hospital. Other scenes at the Ball, where the dancers are stricken by the Red Death, achieved verisimilitude by using pints of realistic stage blood applied by make-up artist George Partleton.

Over $200,000 worth of sets were built for the film at Elstree's Associated British Studios and designed by Art Director Bob Jones to reflect all the grandeur and magnificence of the period.

A dozen or so magnificent antique chandeliers are clustered on the ceilings overlooking the great sweeping staircase of the ballroom. Only once is historical fact broken - and then only briefly - to introduce a specially designed ebony clock which a man of Prospero's visionary power might well have possessed. The timepiece is one of the dominant features of the ballroom set, and is encased in a heavily-carved wooden frame, with a bronze face.

The banqueting tables, at which the Prince and his friends enjoy their gargantuan feast, are weighted by the decorative foods of the time. The guests drink from gold goblets, and gorge themselves on silvered pheasants, loaves of bread fashioned in the shapes of castles, decorated boars' heads, geese, ducks, venison, salmon and blue trout - all by a huge, open, log-burning fireplace.

"The biggest challenge" says Art Director Bob Jones, "Came in creating sets, visualized completely in terms of color, without using any shades in the red spectrum. This dramatically points to the appearance of the Man in Red, representing Death, who arrives towards the end of the film."

Vivid use of color is made, however, in a magnificent and august suite of smaller intercommunicating rooms, in which the complete décor, including flowers, furniture and walls is carried out alternately in white, mauve, yellow and finally black. The mysterious black room is where Prince Prospero and Juliana conduct their diabolical rites of black magic.

On the other studio stages, luxurious sets have been built for the bath scenes in which Francesca is first introduced into the pleasure-loving ways of the Court. Two gilded swans guard a gold sunken bathtub, some twelve feet by nine feet, where the naked and innocent girl is bathing when surprised by Prospero.

Nearby lie the torture chambers built for dungeon scenes showing the dreaded areas of the Palace where Prospero's victims are subdued by force. The chambers were accessorized with thumbscrews, iron maidens, flails, torture chairs and racks - all reserved for those who arouse the displeasure of their Prince.

A complete village of about a hundred thatched houses - an exact replica of an Italian hamlet of the 12th century - was created for burning during the film's opening scenes. After Prospero discovers an outbreak of the Red Death, he commands that the entire village be burnt to the ground with torches. The set, which took two weeks to research, design and build, was used only for about thirty minutes shooting time.

Extensive corridors were built in sections spreading over three stages for scenes in which Francesca runs terrified through the castle. Director Roger Corman explains the psychological motives for the corridors: "If you search for the most chilling moment of any horror film you will usually be able to relate it to a scene in which some character is seen in a long corridor, either running away from, or approaching some unspecified object of unparalleled terror. The moment *before* the revelation of the nature of that 'thing' is what holds the fear."

In "Masque of the Red Death" it is the unexpected sounds of Prospero chanting the black mass, which arouses Francesca from her sleep and prompts her to run, terrified from her room, to find their source. "The frightened figure arouses fear in those watching," says Corman, "and the terrified flight is probably even more alarming in itself than anything which could lie at the end of it."

Director Corman has done considerable research into the psychological reasons behind the popularity of horror films. "They act as a form of therapy," he maintains. "Some physical shape is given to people's vague fears. They survive the terrors and because they are able to live through them and walk out of the cinema at the end of the film, horror pictures can be of great psychological value to many people."

THE MASQUE OF THE RED DEATH
(American-International Pictures)

Produced & Directed by Roger Corman. A James H. Nicholson-Samuel Z. Arloff presentation. Screenplay by Charles Beaumont & R. Wright Campbell, from Edgar Allan Poe's "TheMasque of the Red Death" & "Hop-Frog." Associate Producer: George Willoughby. Music by David Lee. Director of Photography: Nicolas Roeg, B.S.C. (in Panavision & Pathécolor)Production Design by Daniel Haller. Art Direction: Robert Jones. Film Editor: Ann Chegwidden. Camera Operator: Alex Thomson. Sound Recording: Richard Bird & Len Abbott. Sound Editor: Allan Morrison. Choreography by Jack Carter. Set Dresser: Colin Southcott. Costume Supervisor: Laura Nightingale. Make-up: George Partleton. Special Effects: George Blackwell. Titles by Jim Baker. Hairdresser: Elsie Aldon. Assistant Director: Peter Price. Construction Manager: Richard Frift. Script Continuity: Joan Davis. Casting: G.B. Walker. Publicity director: Edna Tromans. An Alta Vista/Anglo Amalgamated Co-Production. Filmed at Elstree Associated British Studios, Borehamwood, Herts, England (for five weeks), beginning November 19, 1963. Released in Los Angeles: June 24, 1964. Released in New York: September 16, 1964. 90 minutes (cut to 84 min. in England).

CAST

Prince Prospero	VINCENT PRICE
Lady Juliana	HAZEL COURT
Francesca	JANE ASHER
Gino	DAVID WESTON
Duke Alfredo	PATRICK MAGEE
Ludovico	NIGEL GREEN
The Man in Red	JOHN WESTBROOK
Hop-Toad	SKIP MARTIN
Esmeralda	VERINA GREENLAW
Signor Veronese (Pig)	JULIAN BURTON
Signorina Escobar (Jackass)	GAYE BROWN
Signor Scarlatti	PAUL WHITSUN-JONES
Signora Scarlatti	JEAN LODGE
Josef, head dungeon guard	ROBERT BROWN
Rodolpho, village elder	DAVID DAVIES
Signor Rimini	HARVEY HALL
Signora Rimini	SARA BRACKETT
Anna-Marie	DOREEN DAWNE
Signor Lampredi (Worm)	BRIAN HEWLETT
Grandmother	GLADYS DAVISON
Dungeon guard	JOHN STONE

www.ingramcontent.com/pod-product-compliance
Lightning Source LLC
Chambersburg PA
CBHW051838020726
47502CB00005B/1840